P9-DCW-377

READERS LOVE LAUREN MYRACLE'S *ttfn*

"Why was i not previously informed that there is a SEQUEL to *ttyl*????? I got *ttfn* in a bookstore yesterday!!! It is SOSO-SOSOSO great!! I'm on page 173 already! I love it. Tons of my buddies read *ttyl* and are lining up 2 borrow it!"
—Katelyn

"I just read *ttfn*, and I loved it! The story seems so real, and I like reading it in text-messages!"—Kaylan

"hey! i absolutely LOVE the *ttyl* series . . . i got the first book on Saturday when i was looking 4 an interesting book 2 read and saw *ttyl*. i read it in 1.5 days!! then i let my bff borrow it and she thought it was great!! well i'm off 2 get the next book!! bye!!" —Haley

"*ttyl* and *ttfn* are the only books i have ever liked! You are an amazing writer . . . I love how your book is written in all instant messages. I love to IM so that's probably one of the reasons it's so much fun to read!" —Molly

ttfn

lauren myracle

Amulet Books
New York

Library of Congress Cataloging-in-Publication Data:
Myracle, Lauren, 1969–

  Ttfn / by Lauren Myracle.

    p. cm.

  Summary: Now high school juniors, Zoe, Maddie, and Angela continue to share "instant messages"
with one another as one of them experiments with drugs, another gets her first boyfriend, and the third
moves three thousand miles away.

  Hardcover ISBN 10: 0-8109-5971-2

  Hardcover ISBN 13: 978-0-8109-5971-2

  Paperback ISBN 10: 0-8109-9279-5

  Paperback ISBN 13: 978-0-8109-9279-5

  [1. Instant messaging—Fiction. 2. Friendship—Fiction. 3. Moving, Household—Fiction. 4. Marijuana—
Fiction. 5. Interpersonal relations—Fiction. 6. High schools—Fiction. 7. Schools—Fiction.] I. Title.
II. Title: Ta-ta for now.
PZ7.M9955Ttf 2006

  [Fic]—dc22

2005015027

First published in hardcover by Amulet Books in 2006.
Copyright © 2006 Lauren Myracle

Printed and bound in U.S.A.
10 9 8 7 6 5 4 3

Design: Interrobang Design Studio

HNA ▌▌▌▌▌

harry n. abrams, inc.

a subsidiary of La Martinière Groupe
115 West 18th Street
New York, NY 10011
www.hnabooks.com

Publisher's Note: This is a work of fiction. Names, characters, places, and incidents are either the product
of the author's imagination or are used fictitiously, and any resemblance to actual persons, living or dead,
business establishments, events, or locales is entirely coincidental.

Every effort has been made to verify Web addresses mentioned in this book. The publisher bears no
responsibility for addresses that have moved or changed.

To all the girlies—and yes! even a few guys!—who shared their IMs with me or emailed me about life in general. Yahootie!!!

Acknowledgments

Oh, li'l dudes, I thank you:

Liz Baltich, Kelly Dean, Todd Mitchell, Laura Pritchett, and Jack Martin, for being the best readers a girl could ask for; Derek DeCoux, poet extraordinaire and all-around cool guy; my agent, Barry Goldblatt, for assuring me that I don't suck whenever I convince myself I do; the groovy folks at Abrams, for giving me such a wonderful book-y home; and the inestimable Susan Van Metre, for making me write the damn novel again and again and AGAIN. *flings self on dagger and perishes*

And thanks to Al, who wanted Maddie to say "blah, blah, blah." (And Jamie and Mirabelle, thank you, too, just for being so cute.)

SnowAngel: hey there, zoe-cakes. r we studs or what?

zoegirl: ya-hootie!

SnowAngel: i have a total adrenaline buzz going, even tho i am completely and thoroughly exhausted. my muscles r gonna be crazy sore tomorrow.

zoegirl: i hear u. can u imagine how in shape we'd be if we did that every day?

SnowAngel: we could call it the winsome-threesome workout-of-the-century. we could make an exercise video and rake in oodles of cash.

zoegirl: even my toenails r tired

SnowAngel: *flops onto pretend bed and groans*

SnowAngel: i told chrissy what we did, and she was like, "u ran up the escalator at peachtree center? that super duper long one?"

zoegirl: the critical point is that we ran up the *down* escalator. u did explain that to her, didn't u?

zoegirl: that's gotta be the longest escalator in the world. seriously, it's as long as a football field.

SnowAngel: i nearly lost it when maddie stopped for a breather and the escalator took her down, down, down. she was all, "noooo! i'm losing ground!"

zoegirl: hee hee

SnowAngel: but in the end we conquered it, cuz we can conquer ANYTHING, baby.

SnowAngel: it's like my new favorite song, "run" by snow patrol. it

1

	goes, "light up, light up, as if u have a choice," and it's all about not giving into the harshness of life even when everything's going against u.
zoegirl:	"as if u have a choice"? sounds sarcastic.
SnowAngel:	no, no, no, it's not. have u heard it?
zoegirl:	is this another of those indie bands u discovered on your "OC" cd?
SnowAngel:	i discovered this one on my own, thank u very much. *pokes out tongue* the song is all melancholy and wistful, but at the same time beautiful and inspiring, and the lead singer's NOT being sarcastic. he's saying, "yeah, the world is hard, and maybe we don't have control, but we should ACT like we do. we should light up inside ourselves and shine."
SnowAngel:	i thoroughly agree, that's all.
zoegirl:	well i do 2
SnowAngel:	and the REASON i shine is cuz of u and mads.
zoegirl:	awwwww
SnowAngel:	it's true. true blue, me and u, and don't forget to add maddie 2.
SnowAngel:	do u like my rhyme?
zoegirl:	very impressive
SnowAngel:	wait, there's more! er, let's c . . . since 7th grade they did not part, they stayed connected in their hearts. zoe's the good girl, maddie's wild, and sweet darling angela is meek and mild.
zoegirl:	meek? hahahahaha! mild? hahahahaha!
SnowAngel:	fine, miss brainiac. U find something to rhyme with wild.
zoegirl:	"and sweet goofy angela tends to act like a child"?

Send   Cancel

SnowAngel:	hey now!
zoegirl:	just teasing. u know i love u.
zoegirl:	i've just got kid-type ppl on my brain, cuz guess what? i got the job at Kidding Around!
SnowAngel:	wh-hoo! *happy dance, happy dance*
zoegirl:	there was a message waiting for me when i got home. i'm psyched.
SnowAngel:	ah, to be wiping noses and chasing toddlers. when do u start?
zoegirl:	um, don't freak, ok?
SnowAngel:	why would i freak? ur not gonna say something to make me freak, r u?
SnowAngel:	wait a minute. don't u DARE tell me u have to start tonite.
zoegirl:	the thing is . . . i do.
SnowAngel:	zoe! noooo!
zoegirl:	saturday nite's their busiest nite. the director wants me to come in for training.
SnowAngel:	but we were gonna watch "A Cinderella Story"! we were gonna freeze-frame the part where Hilary Duff goes into the locker room and has a fight with Chad Michael Murray!
zoegirl:	i know, and i will miss chad very much and pray that he understands. but we can have our "cinderella story" extravaganza tomorrow. that'll be even better, cuz that way maddie can actually join us.
SnowAngel:	the point being that she has plans tonite 2? yeah, rub it in. u've got ur job and maddie has her cousin's wedding and i have a big old pile of poop. thanks a lot.

3

zoegirl:	angela, u r such a drama queen.
SnowAngel:	😩
zoegirl:	ur not really mad, r u?
SnowAngel:	of course i'm mad! *flames shoot from ears*
SnowAngel:	only not really, cuz this way i can watch "extreme makeover: home edition" and no one will be here to make fun of me. and i will cry and it will be very emotional, and if u would just TRY the show then u would c what i mean.
zoegirl:	umm . . . no
zoegirl:	but u know what's weird? and i mean this in the nicest way ever. last year u would have been totally upset if i'd changed our plans at the last minute. i mean, truly upset, with all kinds of wounded hurt feelings. but this year, ur so much more chill. why is that, do u think?
SnowAngel:	cuz i'm a junior, that's why. *struts around in funky junior-ness* cuz i can drive, even tho i don't have a car. cuz i choose to light up, light up, even tho i will be all alone on a saturday nite, and even tho there is seriously something up with my parents, not that they'll admit it.
zoegirl:	there's something up with your parents? explain.
SnowAngel:	it's just this feeling i've been getting.
zoegirl:	like what? and for how long?
SnowAngel:	i dunno, maybe a week?
zoegirl:	a week?! why r u just now telling me???
SnowAngel:	it's like they're hiding something, i can't explain it better than that. i keep thinking that maybe i'm making it up, but then i think that i'm not.

4   Send   Cancel

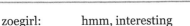

zoegirl:	hmm, interesting
zoegirl:	maybe it's a *good* thing they're hiding—like, that they're taking u to hawaii.
SnowAngel:	i dunno, that somehow doesn't seem very likely.
SnowAngel:	but, whatever. i'm not gonna worry about it, cuz i'm the new and improved Chill Angela. u think they would name a Barbie after me?
zoegirl:	definitely. and for the accessory, she could have a tiny iPod so she could listen to that "light up" song.
SnowAngel:	no, her accessory would be a tiny picture of u, me, and mads, cuz that's why i'm chill for real. cuz no matter what, i've got u guys giving me my me-ness. ☺
zoegirl:	maddie and i don't give u ur you-ness. u give urself ur you-ness.
SnowAngel:	"you-ness." now there's a word for u.
SnowAngel:	my granddad's name was eunice, btw
zoegirl:	grandDAD? u mean ur grandmom.
SnowAngel:	nope, my granddad. only he spelled it "unus."
zoegirl:	ugh. what were his parents trying to do to him?
SnowAngel:	his full name was unus faye. he went by U.F.
zoegirl:	i am so sorry to hear that.
SnowAngel	yep
zoegirl:	well, on that note, gtg. wish me luck on my first day, which is really my first nite!
SnowAngel:	good luck on ur first day which is really ur first nite!
SnowAngel:	ta ta for now!

Send   Cancel

Saturday, November 20, 5:16 PM E.S.T.

SnowAngel: hey, maderoo. getting all dolled up for ur cousin's wedding?

mad maddie: fyi, the dolling is done. fyi, i look fabu.

mad maddie: the pops, however, has hit a new low.

SnowAngel: ooo, do tell

mad maddie: ahem. he bought this self-hair-cutter thing, right? cuz he's such a cheapskate that he didn't wanna fork over 10 bucks at lloyd's barbershop. and of course he decides that today, the day of donovan's wedding, is the perfect day for a trim. so i get home to find dad in the bathroom, hair-cutter aloft, and as i walk to my room, i hear the buzzing begin. bzzzzzzzzzzzzzz.

SnowAngel: what'd he do, give himself a mohawk?

mad maddie: if only. so then the buzzing stops, and he goes, "oops." "what happened?" i yell. and he says, "i put on the wrong attachment. guess my hair will be a little shorter than usual, huh?"

SnowAngel: uh oh

mad maddie: and then for some reason he starts asking if i have a safety pin or a needle or anything pokey. i think he was taking the whole thing apart. but no, i did not have anything pokey, so after a while he puts it back together and the buzzing starts again. and then it shuts off. and he starts LAFFING.

SnowAngel: oh, crap. what happened?

mad maddie: my idiot father forgot to put ANY attachment back on, which meant that when he started up again, he took off

6

	an entire strip of hair down to his scalp. as in, bald. and then once he'd done that, he figured there was nothing to do but complete the scalping.
mad maddie:	**my father is a cue ball, angela.**
SnowAngel:	oh no!
SnowAngel:	that cracks me up that he would laff, tho. that's so ur dad.
mad maddie:	**he was all, "what? it's just hair." the moms is massively annoyed.**
SnowAngel:	if my dad went bald on the day of a wedding, my mom would jump out a window. or push HIM out a window.
mad maddie:	**ah, well. we'll go to the reception and drink away our troubles, cuz that's what my family does. should be a good time.**
SnowAngel:	that blows my mind that u can drink right there with them.
mad maddie:	**it's cuz we're irish. it's the law.**
SnowAngel:	my parents would be like, "u r underage. go sit at the kiddie table." but yours r like, "here, have another beer!"
mad maddie:	**well, they won't be the ones actually giving me beers. they'll leave that to my crazy aunts and uncles. and it won't be beer, it'll be champagne.**
SnowAngel:	la di da
mad maddie:	**and before long uncle duncan will be ranting about the iraqis and aunt teresa will be doing the line dance she learned in 8th grade to michael jackson's "beat it."**
mad maddie:	**i'm telling u, donovan's fiancee has noooooo idea what she's in for.**

Send   Cancel

7

SnowAngel:	sounds fun, tho
mad maddie:	**it definitely won't be boring**
SnowAngel:	do u wish—even just a little—that u and ian were still going out, so he could go with u?
mad maddie:	**not at all. ian is a fleck and i am a plane, high in the sky. that's how over him i am.**
SnowAngel:	swear?
mad maddie:	**ok, maybe not a plane. maybe just a . . . telephone pole.**
SnowAngel:	meaning what?
mad maddie:	**meaning that maybe i do miss him, but what's the point? if ian had wanted to come to donovan's wedding with me, then he shouldn't have broken up with me.**
SnowAngel:	he didn't break up with u. u broke up with him.
mad maddie:	**but only cuz i knew that he was going to. he called me a ball and chain, if u don't recall.**
SnowAngel:	WHAT?!!
SnowAngel:	he did NOT call u a ball and chain. he made that ONE comment about wanting to hang out with his friends more, and u did your porcupine thing where u bristle up over nothing.
mad maddie:	**there was more to it than that 1 comment. it was obvious i was cramping his style.**
SnowAngel:	omg. only u would interpret it like that.
SnowAngel:	it's ok to have feelings, u know. it's even ok to miss ian.
mad maddie:	**thanx for that, Dr. Phil.**
SnowAngel:	he adored u, mads. he would take u back in a heartbeat.

Send   Cancel

mad maddie:	**yeah, well, that boat's already sailed.**
mad maddie:	**that's nice of u to say, tho. u r so good to me.**
SnowAngel:	yup, cuz i luv ya
SnowAngel:	anyway, who knows? maybe tonite u'll meet someone new. maybe u'll meet your future husband!
mad maddie:	**or maybe NOT. i'm not looking for a husband, angela—sheesh!**
SnowAngel:	u never know . . .
SnowAngel:	so zoe got that job at Kidding Around, did u hear?
mad maddie:	**that's such a dorky name, Kidding Around. it's like, "hiya, buddy, watcha up to?" "not much—just kidding around." with everyone slugging each other on the shoulder.**
SnowAngel:	cuz it's a childcare place, for when parents don't have a babysitter or whatever. KIDDING around. get it?
mad maddie:	**der, angela. not gettlng It was never the problem.**
mad maddie:	**yikes, time to motor. old baldie's calling my name.**
SnowAngel:	have fun at the wedding! tell donovan congrats for me! OH, and u and zoe r both coming over tomorrow, ok? we're having Sunday Afternoon Movie Madness.
mad maddie:	**that sounds awesome—only not "A Cinderella Story." i am not watching u freeze-frame the locker room shot for the umpteenth billion time.**
SnowAngel:	we will take a vote
mad maddie:	**fine, we'll take a vote**
SnowAngel:	and my vote counts double since it's my house. ☺ buh-bye!

Send   Cancel

9

ttfn

mad maddie: dude! future hubby alert!

SnowAngel: for real???

mad maddie: no. cute boy, tho. very very cute.

SnowAngel: where r u? is the wedding over?

mad maddie: reception. boy's name = clive.

SnowAngel: CLIVE?

mad maddie: but i call him chive, cuz i = witty. friend of donovan.

SnowAngel: cool—i can't wait to hear more when ur not IMing
from your cell. why r u, anyway? just call me!

mad maddie: can't. lurking behind dessert table.

SnowAngel: maddie, get off the phone and go have fun. or else go
somewhere and CALL me, cuz guess what? i think i
figured out why my parents r being so weird.

mad maddie: spill

SnowAngel: it's zoe who helped me figure it out. she was all,
"maybe what they're hiding is a GOOD thing, angela,"
and i think maybe she's right. i think they're buying
me a car!

mad maddie: holy shit!

SnowAngel: i know!!! they keep talking in these hush-hush quiet
voices, and then they clam up whenever i come in the
room. it's extremely suspicious.

mad maddie: well, rock on

mad maddie: as for me, it's bunny hop time!

Send   Cancel

Sunday, November 21, 11:01 AM E.S.T.

zoegirl:	maddie! ur awake and it's only 11:00! how was the wedding?
mad maddie:	**it was awesome, altho i'm kinda hungover. not terrible, tho.**
zoegirl:	tell me more
mad maddie:	**it was mainly family, so the ceremony wasn't huge, but with my family that's probably a good thing. donovan looked great in his tux, and lisa looked drop-dead gorgeous.**
zoegirl:	yeah? what was her dress like?
mad maddie:	**her dress? i don't know. it was . . . white. NOT frou-frou. for lisa it was perfect, especially cuz she's so tiny. but like, naturally tiny. healthy tiny.**
zoegirl:	did she seem happy? was she glowing? when i fall in love, it's gonna be with someone who makes me glow.
mad maddie:	**ok, excuse me while i barf**
zoegirl:	whoa, u really r hungover
mad maddie:	**uh, no, i was barfing cuz somehow ur channeling angela with this "glowing" shit. why does everyone have to get all mushy when it comes to love?**
zoegirl:	i am *not* channeling angela. u cannot compare me to angela, that is so unfair.
mad maddie:	**i don't know if lisa was glowing, but she smiled a lot, and at the reception she gave me a big hug, which surprised me. i used to think she was snobby, but now i'm wondering if she's just shy.**
mad maddie:	**she's not, like, the coolest girl in the world, but she's the**

	coolest girl for donovan, if that makes sense. i think they're good together.
zoegirl:	well, that's awesome. u can be cynical maddie if u have to be, but i want that someday. i wanna fall in love for real.
mad maddie:	**u don't consider mr. h for real?**
zoegirl:	don't, maddie. i don't even like to joke about that.
mad maddie:	**about what? about the fact that u almost had an affair with your horny english teacher?**
zoegirl:	i am covering my ears now. la la la.
mad maddie:	**how about his whole christianity kick, can i joke about that? ya gotta admit, it's great material. it's not very often that a guy uses God to try and lure in the girls.**
zoegirl:	please stop
mad maddie:	**zo, it happened over a year ago. it's ancient history. when WILL i be allowed to joke about it?**
zoegirl:	*never*
zoegirl:	let's change the subject. i talked to angela this morning, and she said u met some guy named after a seasoning. cilantro? paprika?
mad maddie:	**ha ha. it's clive. i just call him chive. he goes to northside.**
zoegirl:	what grade's he in?
mad maddie:	**he's a junior. he loves music, which is why he goes to n'side since they have such a good performing arts department. i told him how i wanna major in music AND advertising and then be the person who makes CD covers.**
mad maddie:	**we talked forever—he's got GORGEOUS eyes—and then we ended up macking in the corner. the moms totally**

Send   Cancel

	caught us, which believe me was completely embarrassing.
zoegirl:	oh god
mad maddie:	**but she was wasted 2, so she didn't care. she got all teary and started saying stuff like, "u and clive! it's meant to be!" and i was like, "mom, no. i love being single." and she goes, "r u telling me ur a slut?"**
zoegirl:	nuh uh
mad maddie:	**then she calls out to all my aunts and uncles in this really loud voice, "someone bring me another drink—my little girl's a slut!"**
zoegirl:	i swear, maddie, your family is so incredibly different from mine. there is no way in the world i would ever have a convo like that with my mother.
mad maddie:	**cuz your family is normal**
mad maddie:	**she was just joking, tho. she was just being wild.**
zoegirl:	was chive around for all that? did he hear your mom call u a slut?
mad maddie:	**yeah, and he laffed. that's the cool thing about him.**
zoegirl:	huh
mad maddie:	**i had FUN, zo. the whole nite was fun. i know it's not your style, but i had a blast.**
zoegirl:	so r u gonna c him again?
mad maddie:	**who, chive? i hope so, yeah, but not in a date-y way if that's what ur asking.**
zoegirl:	why not in a date-y way, if u liked him so much?
mad maddie:	**cuz i'm not looking for that. we don't all have to GLOW, zo. we really don't.**

mad maddie:	**hey, how was your first nite at Kidding Around?**
zoegirl:	i *love* it. the kids r so cute. there was this one little boy, he was maybe 3, and he had all these fake tattoos on his arm. i would point to one and say, "so what's that?" and he'd say, "a snake, but not a *real* snake." or "a bat, but not a *real* bat." or "a lightning, but not a *real* lightning, cuz if it was real lightning, there would be thunder. only not here. somewhere else. where the indians r."
mad maddie:	**what indians?**
zoegirl:	beats me.
zoegirl:	oh—and guess who works there with me?!
mad maddie:	**who?**
zoegirl:	doug schmidt!
mad maddie:	**doug? as in angela's doug?**
zoegirl:	well, he's not really angela's doug, seeing as how she's not the slightest bit interested. but yeah. i was like, "doug! wow!"
mad maddie:	**he's gonna be all over u, i can c it now. he's gonna use u as an inside link. cuz angela may not be interested, but it's a sure bet he's still crushing on her.**
zoegirl:	maybe. i don't know. i just think it's cool that a guy would take a job there in the 1st place.
mad maddie:	**what'd angela say when u told her?**
zoegirl:	we didn't talk about it much, cuz she was kinda distracted. she thinks her parents r buying her a car.
mad maddie:	**oh yeah, that's right—and she says U planted the idea.**
zoegirl:	i did not! i just said she shouldn't assume that whatever's going on with her parents is bad.

14

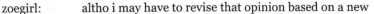

zoegirl:	altho i may have to revise that opinion based on a new and not-so-good development. *don't* tell angela.
mad maddie:	**don't tell angela what?**
zoegirl:	i saw her dad at starbucks this morning. i was getting cappuccinos for my parents cuz i'm such a good daughter, and there was mr. silver. and he wasn't alone.
mad maddie:	**who was he with?**
zoegirl:	a woman, wearing a tailored skirt and blouse. the kind of woman who actually uses lip liner.
mad maddie:	**lip liner, that's hardcore.**
mad maddie:	**so what r u saying?**
zoegirl:	nothing, i'm not saying anything
mad maddie:	**u don't think he's having an affair, do u???**
zoegirl:	no no no, i'm sure he's not.
zoegirl:	i just got a weird vibe, that's all.
mad maddie:	**weird how?**
zoegirl:	u know how normally mr. silver's so friendly and buddy-buddy? well, today when i went over to say hi, he looked really uncomfortable. all brusque and at the same time blushing, like he'd been caught in the act.
mad maddie:	**WHAT act?**
zoegirl:	i dunno. and he didn't introduce me to the lip liner woman, even tho she was smiling very pleasantly like "oh, and who's your little friend?" it was 1 of those moments where he *should* have introduced us, but he didn't.
zoegirl:	there was something suspicious about it. it made me worry that
zoegirl:	never mind
mad maddie:	**what?**

Send   Cancel

15

zoegirl:	it's stupid. it's superstitious. but like, things r going *so well* for us. ur happy, angela's happy, i'm happy. and then i think, shit, when's the bad thing gonna happen, u know?
mad maddie:	**and u think the bad thing has to do with angela's dad and the lip liner woman?**
zoegirl:	i didn't say that
mad maddie:	**anywayz, ur crazy. enuff bad stuff happened to us last year to last a lifetime.**
zoegirl:	tell me about it. let's c, 1st there was me and mr. h, then angela and all her boy probs, and then as if that wasn't enuff, u went all psycho with your terrible jana obsession.
mad maddie:	**"obsession"? that's a bit of an exaggeration, wouldn't u say?**
zoegirl:	no. u were like her clone. u started to talk like her, dress like her . . .
zoegirl:	i am *so* glad ur over that, btw
mad maddie:	**listen, pal. if i'm not allowed to mention mr. h, then ur not allowed to bring up jana.**
zoegirl:	fine, then u know how i feel.
zoegirl:	but don't u c the pattern? it was last year right around thanksgiving that all hell broke loose, and now here we r, right around thanksgiving again.
mad maddie:	**nooooo, zoe. it was BEFORE last thanksgiving that all hell broke loose, cuz over thanksgiving itself, we were blissing out on cumberland island. or have u forgotten?**
zoegirl:	of course i haven't forgotten!

16   Send   Cancel

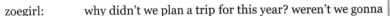

zoegirl:	why didn't we plan a trip for this year? weren't we gonna make it a tradition?
mad maddie:	**oops, 2 late now**
zoegirl:	c! that's what's making me feel this way. we're 2 complacent, just going along like everything's fine.
mad maddie:	**yeahhhh, cuz everything IS fine.**
mad maddie:	**don't worry, zo. life is good, and ain't nothin gonna change. c ya at angela's!**

Sunday, November 21, 7:42 PM E.S.T.

SnowAngel:	zoe! it's been eons since i saw u—almost a whole hour! u left your sweatshirt, btw.
zoegirl:	bring it to me tomorrow, will ya?
zoegirl:	is maddie still there?
SnowAngel:	she just left, after patching the butt of her jeans with duct tape cuz she realized they were ripped. it cracks me up, this "i'm such a crazy-ass" stage she's in.
zoegirl:	like at donovan's wedding?
zoegirl:	it blows my mind that her mom would call her a slut and she would think it's funny.
SnowAngel:	she said her mom was drunk, tho
zoegirl:	which makes it even more mind-blowing. do U get drunk with YOUR mom?
SnowAngel:	hahaha. my mom would be the one marching around and slapping drinks out of people's hands.
zoegirl:	i love maddie's mom, it goes w/o saying. and of course i love maddie. i just worry about her sometimes.

Send   Cancel   17

SnowAngel:	oh well, guess she knows what she's doing.
SnowAngel:	so what'd u think about chive?
zoegirl:	he sounds cool, i suppose. i need to meet him before i decide.
SnowAngel:	i wish she was still going out with ian.
zoegirl:	i know. ian is such a good guy.
zoegirl:	u think they'll ever get back together?
SnowAngel:	no, cuz u know how maddie is. when she gets hurt, that's it. there's no looking back. and ian really hurt her, even tho he didn't mean to.
zoegirl:	and even tho she'll never admit it out loud. she's so funny that way, always having to be so tough.
SnowAngel:	like with chive and the whole mack-and-run incident, u mean?
zoegirl:	exactly. i know maddie thinks that's fine—the typical maddie it's-no-big-deal approach—but sometimes i think she's, like, putting up a front. i mean, when u fool around with somebody, it has to mean *something* doesn't it?
SnowAngel:	u would think, yeah
zoegirl:	she and i talked about that at your house, actually. it was while u were downstairs searching for the dvd. i think i maybe said some things i shouldn't have.
SnowAngel:	ooo, like what?
zoegirl:	like that i don't agree with the whole friends-with-benefits philosophy. like i think that works out great for guys, but not so much for girls.
SnowAngel:	i completely agree
zoegirl:	but i'm worried i came off a little harsh. i just kept talking and talking, and all these words came out of my

	mouth w/o my really meaning them to. somehow being with maddie just brings that out in me.
SnowAngel:	oh well, live and learn.
SnowAngel:	so hey, did u notice my parents and how freaky-deaky they're being? they're thoroughly hiding something. it is so obvious.
zoegirl:	huh
zoegirl:	well, whatever it is, i wouldn't worry about it.
SnowAngel:	???
SnowAngel:	what happened to "i'm sure it's something good" and "maybe they're taking u to hawaii!"
zoegirl:	nothing, it's just
SnowAngel:	just WHAT?
zoegirl:	ok, fine. your dad *did* seem a little off.
SnowAngel:	how so? tell me, tell me, tell me.
zoegirl:	i dunno. like he didn't wanna meet anyone's eyes, does that make sense? and he didn't stick around and tease us the way he usually does.
zoegirl:	i guess he just seemed strung-out.
SnowAngel:	cuz it is no doubt very exhausting doing price comparisons b/w PT Cruisers and VW bugs. omigod— do u think he's getting me a bug?!!
zoegirl:	er . . . i'm not sure that was the vibe i was picking up.
SnowAngel:	if i got a bug, i could put a daisy in that little flower-holder thing. i think that is so cute, how they come with their own little vases.
SnowAngel:	but a used car would be ok 2. ANY car would be ok. then i wouldn't have to rely on u and maddie all the time.

Send   Cancel

zoegirl:	i know i said to stay positive, but what if it's not a car?
SnowAngel:	what, now u think it's something bad after all? like that my parents r getting a divorce, or that my dad's got cancer?
zoegirl:	angela, no! i'm sure it's not that!
SnowAngel:	it's not like those thoughts haven't crossed my mind. i overheard my mom talking to my aunt sadie on the phone, and she was saying things like, "i'm completely overwhelmed" and "don't know how we'll tell the girls."
zoegirl:	oh shit, angela
zoegirl:	did she mention anything about . . . anything else?
SnowAngel:	anything else like what?
zoegirl:	oh look—maddie just popped up on my buddy list. hold on, ok? i'll be right back!
SnowAngel:	zoe!!! u r supposed to be talking to ME, not maddie!
SnowAngel:	get back here this instant!!!!

Sunday, November 21, 7:59 PM E.S.T.

zoegirl:	maddie, thank god! angela's all freaked about her parents—she brought it up, not me—and i feel really weird about the whole starbucks encounter. should i tell her about seeing her dad with the lip liner woman?
mad maddie:	**shit, don't ask me**
zoegirl:	i'm sure it's nothing, but at the same time i don't want to be the 1 to bring it up.
mad maddie:	**then don't**

20

zoegirl:	but if it was *my* dad, i'd want to know.
zoegirl:	i think.
mad maddie:	**u think 2 much, zoe. that's your problem.**
zoegirl:	ur right, ur right. no need to worry angela over something that could be nothing until we find out for sure!

Sunday, November 21, 8:04 PM E.S.T.

zoegirl:	hey there, i'm back
SnowAngel:	u r on my bad list *glowers fiercely*
SnowAngel:	i can't believe u'd abandon me like that when my father could very well have a deadly disease!
zoegirl:	i'm 99 percent sure your dad doesn't have a deadly disease. really, i am.
SnowAngel:	so what's going on with maddie, who's apparently so much more important than me?
zoegirl:	please. she had a bio question.
SnowAngel:	???
SnowAngel:	u guys aren't in the same class.
zoegirl:	i know, but mr. mack uses the same exact lesson plans. boring boring.
SnowAngel:	anyway, i'm taking bio too. why didn't she ask ME her question?
zoegirl:	u poor thing! ur having a hard day, aren't u?
SnowAngel:	yes *sniff, sniff*
zoegirl:	oh, angela. u better go have some chocolate, or better yet some ben & jerry's. and u probably better spend some time with chad michael murray again 2.

SnowAngel:	perhaps i will. in bed with my bunny slippers on and a drop of lavender oil on my pulse points for relaxation.
zoegirl:	very good idea
SnowAngel:	*takes deep calming breath. takes deep calming breath again*
SnowAngel:	bye!

Sunday, November 21, 8:10 PM E.S.T.

SnowAngel:	it COULD still be a car, couldn't it? my dad could be strung-out about car payments . . . couldn't he?
zoegirl:	angela, put it out of your mind. ur gonna drive yourself crazy. now go get that new york super fudge chunk!
SnowAngel:	ok, ok. good nite!

Monday, November 22, 4:17 PM E.S.T.

SnowAngel:	*stomps into bedroom and plunks down in front of computer*
SnowAngel:	am i a happy camper? no, i am not. care to hazard a guess at why?
zoegirl:	er . . . did something happen when u got home from school?
SnowAngel:	i caught my mom talking to my aunt sadie AGAIN, and in front of her on the coffee table was an empty container of maple pecans, which she only eats when she's stressed. so i confronted her, and she finally admitted that something's going on.
zoegirl:	she did? whoa.

zoegirl:	did she say it has to do with . . . life changes?
SnowAngel:	life changes?
SnowAngel:	omg, do u think my mom's going thru MENOPAUSE?
zoegirl:	menopause?! no, i was talking more about . . . life changes in general. when ppl, u know, change.
zoegirl:	but that doesn't matter. just tell me what she said!
SnowAngel:	*groans in a loud and aggrieved way*
SnowAngel:	what she SAID is that she didn't wanna talk about it w/o my dad and chrissy. so we're going to dinner tomorrow nite, and they'll tell us then. chrissy and i get to pick the place—anywhere we want.
zoegirl:	anywhere u wanna go? oh no!
SnowAngel:	what?
zoegirl:	nothing, it's just that this is so after-school special. parents *always* let the kids pick the restaurant when they're about to give bad news.
zoegirl:	remember that one about the girl whose parents were getting divorced, and her friend was like, "don't pick mcdonald's, cuz then u'll never wanna go there again. pick some place u really hate." and so she picked a chinese restaurant and ended up getting sick all over the table?
SnowAngel:	i'm not picking mcdonalds, and i'm not picking chinese. i'm sorry, but i'm picking some place really good, cuz if they're gonna give us bad news, they're gonna have to do it over a super nice meal.
zoegirl:	ah, good strategy
SnowAngel:	oh god
SnowAngel:	i'm probably not getting a car, am i? ☹
zoegirl:	well . . .

Send   Cancel

23

SnowAngel: i'm gonna call maddie. i have to tell her what's going on.

zoegirl: chin up, angela. just remember: everyone loves u no matter what!

Tuesday, November 23, 7:31 PM E.S.T.

mad maddie: **hola, zo. ever since i got home from school i've been thinking about angela. u figure she's left for her big family dinner?**

zoegirl: she's probably in the middle of it this very second.

zoegirl: i'm worried.

mad maddie: **i had the craziest thought about what might be going on. forget the mr. silver's-having-an-affair theory: what if angela's mom is preggers?!!**

zoegirl: what???

mad maddie: **she's not THAT old, u know. she could have some eggs left. and maybe the woman mr. silver was talking to was just a friend, someone he could spill his guts to. and that's why he looked so nervous, cuz he didn't know what u'd overheard.**

zoegirl: oh, man, angela would *freak* if her mom's pregnant.

mad maddie: **it would explain all the hush-hush-ness**

zoegirl: ur right, it would

mad maddie: **and i really don't think mr. silver's the type to have an affair, do u?**

zoegirl: i'd be so sad if he was. it would be so depressing.

mad maddie: **we'll know soon enuff, i guess**

mad maddie: **in other news, i may be crippled for life. u may have to call me gimpy. or the gimpster.**

Send   Cancel

zoegirl:	huh?
mad maddie:	**i was taking a shower and the conditioner was all at the bottom of the bottle, so i turned it upside down and shook it and it flew out of my hand and hit my foot. it totally cut my toe open. blood was, llke, swirling down the drain.**
zoegirl:	owww!
mad maddie:	**"death by conditioner." i can c the obituary now.**
zoegirl:	"instead of flowers, the family has requested donations to aveda."
mad maddie:	**ha. only i'm a paul mitchell girl.**
zoegirl:	paul mitchell doesn't lather
mad maddie:	**it does if ur not afraid to slab it on. u gotta be fearless, girl.**
mad maddie:	**IM me if u hear anything from angela!**

Tuesday, November 23, 8:03 PM E.S.T.

SnowAngel:	call my cell! now!
zoegirl:	r u at the restaurant?
SnowAngel:	yes. call me!!!

Tuesday, November 23, 8:25 PM E.S.T.

zoegirl:	maddie, ur not gonna believe this.
mad maddie:	**believe what? did u talk to angela?**
zoegirl:	just now on her cell, and she is beyond upset.
zoegirl:	maddie, her dad's not having an affair—he lost his job.
mad maddie:	**he what?**

Send   Cancel

25

zoegirl:	he was *fired*. isn't that terrible?
mad maddie:	**WHY?**
zoegirl:	i don't know. "downsizing" is what her dad told her.
mad maddie:	**omg**
zoegirl:	and get this: it happened over a month ago. mrs. silver knew, but not angela and chrissy.
mad maddie:	**he's been hiding it this whole time?**
mad maddie:	**it's so dumb when grown-ups do that. don't they know it always makes things worse?**
zoegirl:	tell me about it . . .
mad maddie:	**so who was the mystery woman at starbucks?**
zoegirl:	well, i asked angela that—altho i didn't mention the affair part, so don't u either. and angela said it was probably his career counselor. he's, like, got to start his life all over again. doesn't that seem unfair?
mad maddie:	**whoa**
mad maddie:	**so what's he gonna do?**
zoegirl:	i don't know. angela couldn't talk long cuz she had to get back to the table, but she said she'll IM us when she gets home.
mad maddie:	**man oh man**
zoegirl:	i *told* u something bad was gonna happen, remember? i told u things couldn't go on being so great forever.
mad maddie:	**jesus. i guess u were right!**

Tuesday, November 23, 9:20 PM E.S.T.

SnowAngel:	my life is hell—complete and utter hell!!!

mad maddie:	**i know, angela. I'm so sorry.**
SnowAngel:	no, u DON'T know. it's so much worse. i can't even talk, cuz i'm crying so hard. i can't even keep my fingers on the stupid keyboard!
mad maddie:	**what's going on? WHAT'S worse?**
SnowAngel:	i'm not telling it twice, so just click on the stupid chatroom!

You have just entered the room "Angela's Boudoir."
mad maddie has entered the room.

SnowAngel:	zoe? u here?

zoegirl has entered the room.

zoegirl:	i'm here. wassup?
SnowAngel:	there's no other way to say it, so i just will.
SnowAngel:	my dad's making us move to california!!!
zoegirl:	*what*?
SnowAngel:	i hate my parents. i hate everyone! why is this happening?!!!
mad maddie:	**ur moving to CALIFORNIA???**
mad maddie:	**NOOOOOO. angela, that's crazy!**
zoegirl:	u *can't* move! u . . . u can't!
SnowAngel:	well apparently i can, cuz i'm a TEENAGER and i have no control over my life! i have to do what my stupid PARENTS say, even if it's the most horrible thing in the entire world!

Send   Cancel

27

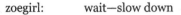

ttfn

zoegirl:	wait—slow down
zoegirl:	your dad lost his job, and that majorly majorly sucks. but how did we get from there to california???
SnowAngel:	cuz all this time when my dad's SUPPOSEDLY been at work, he's actually been meeting with his career counselor and filling out on-line applications. that's how!
mad maddie:	**zoe thought your dad was having an affair, btw**
SnowAngel:	WHAT???
mad maddie:	**she did. she thought the career counselor was his lover.**
zoegirl:	maddie!!!
SnowAngel:	i don't care. i wish the career counselor WAS his lover, cuz believe me, that would be better than the truth.
SnowAngel:	he applied to this one company in el cerrito, and they offered him a position. they want him to start right away!
zoegirl:	el cerrito? where's el cerrito?
mad maddie:	**angela, listen to me. forget el cerrito, forget your dad's career counselor lover. U R NOT ALLOWED TO MOVE.**
mad maddie:	**your dad hasn't said yes, has he?**
SnowAngel:	he hasn't accepted the job YET, but he's flying us out to look at housing. that's his whole thing, that he wants chrissy and me to at least see el cerrito before we make up our minds against it. we're going over thanksgiving!
mad maddie:	**THANKSGIVING?!!**
zoegirl:	angela, please tell me ur kidding. thanksgiving is this thursday!
SnowAngel:	we're having turkey at my aunt sadie's at 11:00, and

Send   Cancel

then we're catching a 3:30 flight to california. our meal won't even be digested by then! it's insane!!!

zoegirl: i can't believe they just *sprung* this on u like this. this is so awful!

SnowAngel: i know! dad was all, "we didn't want to worry u w/o reason, we wanted to work out the details." and i was like, "were u EVER gonna tell us, or were u just gonna stick us on a plane and be like, 'good-bye, old life. hello, el cerrito!'"

SnowAngel: crap, i can't do this. my hands are shaking. my whole body is shaking.

mad maddie: want us to come over?

SnowAngel: will u?

mad maddie: of course, and we'll figure out how to beat this. we will, angela. CUZ U R NOT MOVING TO CALIFORNIA.

SnowAngel: what about u, zoe? will your mom let u out of the house this late?

zoegirl: i'll lie to her if i have to—i'll tell her i have to go buy new highlighters.

SnowAngel: well, come quick

mad maddie: we're on the way!!!

Wednesday, November 24, 4:30 PM E.S.T.

mad maddie: god, zoe, poor angela. she was like a zombie today, wandering around school with that beat-up expression on her face.

zoegirl: i know, i feel *terrible*

Send   Cancel

mad maddie:	**yeah, i could tell. every time i saw u, u gave me the most awful look.**
zoegirl:	that wasn't cuz of angela. that's cuz i'm still mad at u about the whole mr. silver thing. i can't believe u told her i thought her dad was having an affair!
mad maddie:	**i'm sorry i'm sorry i'm sorry. how many times must i apologize?**
mad maddie:	**but c'mon, angela knew not to take it seriously. she's good that way.**
zoegirl:	she's good *every* way
zoegirl:	i can't live w/o her, mads. i can't even imagine it.
mad maddie:	**i can't either. but i thought about it on my way home, and i have an idea. the silvers will fly to california tomorrow, and angela will tell her dad she hates el cerrito, and that'll be the end of it. cuz mr. silver can't say no to angela, right?**
zoegirl:	i don't know. he sure has said no to her before. like when she wanted to build a fire pit in their backyard, remember?
mad maddie:	**just so we could roast marshmallows, which is such an angela kind of thing to wanna do.**
zoegirl:	and then we roasted them anyway in the oven, and the pot holder caught on fire and mr. silver had a fit. poor angela!
mad maddie:	**AAARGH, my head hurts. we have to talk about something else or i'm gonna explode.**
mad maddie:	**did i tell u i almost found a googlewhack?**
zoegirl:	???
mad maddie:	**it's my distraction therapy. u go to google and u type 2**

	words into the search area, and the goal is to get only 1 hit. for example, "toking marsupials."
zoegirl:	toking marsupials?
mad maddie:	**or "phlegmatic weepies" or "crampy dailiness." or my fave, "crapulent porker."**
mad maddie:	**those aren't mine, tho. i can't take credit for them.**
zoegirl:	huh. pity.
mad maddie:	**it's extremely hard to find a true googlewhack, but i came close. "flatulent madigan" got 60 hits, while "absorbent madigan" got 636. but "madigan's pantaloons" only got 3.**
zoegirl:	distraction therapy, u say?
mad maddie:	**3, i tell u! this is muy impressive!**
zoegirl:	i'm not sure i'm grasping the point of all this . . .
mad maddie:	**the point is that there IS no point. it keeps me from thinking about angela, that's all.**
mad maddie:	**but since U made me think about her again—thanks a lot—do u think she's coming to dylan's party tonite?**
zoegirl:	i don't know. she's pretty depressed.
mad maddie:	**yeah, which is exactly why she needs to come.**
mad maddie:	**what about u?**
zoegirl:	i have to work first—i picked up a shift since we have tomorrow off. but i'll swing by after.
mad maddie:	**ooo, at Kidding Around? nudge, nudge, know what i mean, know what i mean?**
zoegirl:	maddie, ur like trying to make a sex joke about a childcare facility.
mad maddie:	**it's a stupid name. i can't help it.**

Send   Cancel

31

mad maddie:	**so should i invite chive to dylan's? i wanna invite him to do SOMETHING, only i don't want it to be boring, which i'm fairly sure dylan's won't be. have u checked out his xanga recently?**
zoegirl:	whose? chive's?
mad maddie:	**dylan's, dummy**
zoegirl:	oh. yeah, it makes me wanna buy him hooked on phonics.
mad maddie:	**HA. what i meant, however, is that there will be copious amounts of beer.**
zoegirl:	dylan's an idiot to post that on the web. does he not think his parents will find it?
zoegirl:	tonnie wyndham's in my english class, and last week she posted on her blog how she'd plagiarized some book review. only ms. griffith found out, cuz ms. griffith surfs the net and types in her students' names.
mad maddie:	**tonnie is a case. today in health, she asked how many calories r in a tablespoon of sperm.**
zoegirl:	ewww!
mad maddie:	**wanna know the answer? 9**
zoegirl:	that is revolting. mrs. wayker actually knew?
mad maddie:	**guess it's not the first time it's come up.**
mad maddie:	**ha—come up, get it?**
zoegirl:	i am *never* giving anyone a blow job, not even my husband.
mad maddie:	**bullshit. u totally will.**
zoegirl:	why would u say that? it's disgusting.
mad maddie:	**prude, prude, prude. when u find the person who makes u GLOW, u'll go down on him quick as a wink. and then HE'LL glow. you'll blow; he'll glow.**

Send   Cancel

mad maddie: god, i'm on a roll. this stuff just comes out of me—i don't even have to try.

zoegirl: maddie, there's nothing here for u to be proud of. hate to break it to u.

mad maddie: blah blah blah. i'm gonna make the bold move and call chive, and then i'll IM angela and tell her that she's required to go, 2.

mad maddie: byeas!

Wednesday, November 24, 5:41 PM E.S.T.

mad maddie: hey, girl. ready for dylan's party?

SnowAngel: dylan's party? that's tonite?

mad maddie: yeah, and ur coming. and so is chive! wh-hoo! so u'll get to meet him, which u claim u've been wanting to do.

mad maddie: don't say no, cuz u need to get out. u've been moping about in your room ever since u got home from school, haven't u?

SnowAngel: hmm . . . yes and no. i was moping for a while, but it wasn't helping, and all i could think about was how terrible everything is. so i rode my bike to little five points to clear my head.

mad maddie: huh, exercise. not familiar with the concept.

mad maddie: did it work?

SnowAngel: well, it's not like i'm leaping up and down for joy, but i don't feel QUITE so suicidal anymore.

SnowAngel: wanna know why?

mad maddie: er . . . why?

SnowAngel:	cuz of what happened when i got back home, which i am calling my GREAT BRACELET BREAKTHROUGH. *strikes a tragically romantic pose* even in these darkest of times, i found a light at the end of the tunnel.
mad maddie:	**angela, what the hell r u talking about?**
SnowAngel:	i parked my bike when i got to little five points, and i did a little window shopping. and i found a bracelet that i love sooooo much. it's made out of brown leather, and the ends connect with a silver clasp, and on the front there's a slender silver rectangle with the word "believe" etched onto it.
SnowAngel:	i know ur gonna say it's corny, but it's like fate was jumping out at me and telling me that everything's gonna be all right. telling me to BELIEVE.
mad maddie:	**oh, angela. ur not gonna start carrying around little pewter angels, r u? or those stones that say "joy" or "happiness" or—god help us—"believe"?**
SnowAngel:	don't u WANT me to believe?
SnowAngel:	why r u making fun of me when i'm actually feeling the tiniest bit better?
mad maddie:	**i'm not making fun of U. i'm making fun of those dorky stones.**
SnowAngel:	back to my bracelet. in order to look right, it has to be fastened nice and snug, cuz otherwise the "believe" part rotates around where it's not supposed to. i was able to get it PRETTY tight, but not just-right tight, cuz it kept slipping out of place just when i thought i had it.

34

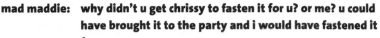
mad maddie: **why didn't u get chrissy to fasten it for u? or me? u could have brought it to the party and i would have fastened it for u.**

SnowAngel: cuz it became, like, this big thing. cuz in my head i was like, "am i the kind of person who gives up? no. am i the kind of person who fights to the end? yes."

mad maddie: **over a bracelet?**

SnowAngel: here is what i finally did, and i think i should get a patent cuz it was so brilliant. i hooked one of my necklaces to the end of the bracelet to give me more slack, and then i used my teeth to pull the necklace tight, which in turn pulled the bracelet tight. then i used my free hand to reach around and fasten the clasp—effortlessly, i tell u!—and voila, my bracelet is on and gorgeous. and every time i look at it, i just think about how things CAN work out if u make them. isn't that good?

mad maddie: **well, lord love a duck**

SnowAngel: i know i have to get on that stupid plane tomorrow, but we haven't moved YET. i just have to believe.

mad maddie: **does this mean u'll come to the party?**

SnowAngel: can u give me a ride?

mad maddie: **yahoo! i'll pick u up in an hour!**

Wednesday, November 24, 6:30 PM E.S.T.

zoegirl: hey, angela. i'm IMing from work, so i've gotta be quick. i'm not supposed to be on the computer.

SnowAngel: hey, girl. does this mean ur not coming to dylan's?

zoegirl:	no, i am, just not till after work.
zoegirl:	listen, i just wanted to say . . . well, i'm sorry i thought your dad was having an affair.
SnowAngel:	oh yeahhhhhh. THAT.
zoegirl:	i don't know why i even thought that. pretty stupid, huh?
SnowAngel:	don't worry about it. i told my dad, tho.
zoegirl:	u told your *dad*?
zoegirl:	omg. did u tell him it was me who said it?
SnowAngel:	of course. i said it to get back at him for all the crap he's putting me thru, but it backfired cuz he just laffed. my mom thought it was pretty funny, 2.
zoegirl:	angela!
SnowAngel:	they said to tell u they have a very fulfilling sex life. aren't u glad u brought it up?
zoegirl:	this is so embarrassing! i can't believe u *told* them!!!
SnowAngel:	oh well
SnowAngel:	c ya at dylan's!

Thursday, November 25, 11:45 AM E.S.T.

mad maddie:	**good morning to u on this lovely day of giving thanks, which would be far lovelier if not for the taste of sour beer wafting about my tonsils.**
mad maddie:	**ooo, baby, can u say cotton-mouth?**
zoegirl:	hi, mads. still recovering from last nite?
mad maddie:	**that was so much fun. i kissed chive on the washing machine, did i tell u?**
zoegirl:	yes, maddie. u called me from your cell phone even tho i

Send   Cancel

	was 20 feet away in the living room having a very nice convo with doug, which u interrupted. u were all, "i'm kissing chive on the washing machine! hahaha, isn't that hilarious? i'm kissing chive on the washing machine!"
mad maddie:	**cuz u r my friend. cuz i wanna share my life with u.**
zoegirl:	and then u made chive talk to me. it was very random and unnecessary.
mad maddie:	**i did not make chive talk to u.**
mad maddie:	**did i?**
zoegirl:	do u not remember? doug and i talked about how much we hate it when people do that. "here, talk to my great-aunt zelda." "here, talk to my buddy from camp whom u've never met and never will."
mad maddie:	**well, what did u say to chive on the phone? what did HE say?**
zoegirl:	he was surprisingly nice, given that i'm sure he wanted to be forced on me just as much as i wanted to be forced on him. he was like, "let's c, ur the shy 1, right?"
zoegirl:	maddie, did u tell him i was shy?
mad maddie:	**i dunno, i might have**
zoegirl:	why?
mad maddie:	**what do u mean, why? cuz ur my bud.**
mad maddie:	**i told him all about angela, 2**
zoegirl:	well, that's very sweet, but please don't go around telling ppl i'm shy.
mad maddie:	**but u R shy**
zoegirl:	yeah, but it made me feel dumb
mad maddie:	**chive made u feel dumb?**

Send Cancel

37

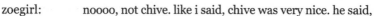

zoegirl:	noooo, not chive. like i said, chive was very nice. he said, "hey now, nothing wrong with being shy. just don't be afraid to let loose, k? u can't always stand around with ur hands in your pockets. sometimes u gotta bust a funky move!"
mad maddie:	**ha, like that'll ever happen**
mad maddie:	**so did u like him? don't u think he's awesome?**
zoegirl:	i did like him. he had that drunk-and-sincere thing going on, but he was definitely charming.
mad maddie:	**he's cute, 2. more like gorgeous.**
zoegirl:	especially his eyes
zoegirl:	but, ahem, what's going on here? i thought u and he were just friends.
mad maddie:	**we r!**
mad maddie:	**what, u think i wanna be his girlfriend?**
zoegirl:	doug assumed u were. he saw the 2 of u together, and he said it looked like u were really into each other.
mad maddie:	**that's just chive. he does this deep gaze thing when ur talking to him, as if ur the only thing that matters.**
zoegirl:	well, i guess that's why doug thought u were a couple.
mad maddie:	**doug, doug, doug. why the obsession with doug all of a sudden? anywayz, the 2 of u hung out for the whole party, but that doesn't make U a couple, now does it?**
zoegirl:	hanging out versus hanging all over . . .
zoegirl:	jk!
mad maddie:	**i'm gonna let that slide, cuz at least i'm getting some.**
zoegirl:	ick, maddie!!!
mad maddie:	**it was cool that doug came, tho. i don't usually c him at those parties.**

Send   Cancel

zoegirl:	well, we were chatting at work and i told him about it.
mad maddie:	**i liked his shirt**
zoegirl:	"tough guys wear pink"? he wore it on purpose for the kids at Kidding Around. graham especially. graham's that 3-yr-old i told u about, remember?
zoegirl:	last week graham wore pink socks, and a girl named ashleigh told him that only girls r allowed to wear pink.
mad maddie:	**alas, it starts so young**
zoegirl:	graham is adorable, btw. i call him graham cracker.
mad maddie:	**bet he's never heard that in all his 3 yrs**
zoegirl:	last nite i played candyland with him, and i let him land on queen frostine even tho that wasn't the card he drew. he said, "ur the best, zoe." he kept saying it over and over. "ur the best."
mad maddie:	**awwww**
mad maddie:	**so i thought angela did pretty well with the whole party thing, didn't u?**
zoegirl:	remarkably well. freakily well, given all that's going on.
mad maddie:	**no doubt cuz of THE BRACELET**
zoegirl:	ah, yes, *the bracelet*
mad maddie:	**but now she's having her thanksgiving dinner at eleven in the frickin morning and preparing to jet off to california. isn't that just wrong?**
zoegirl:	i hate it. it makes me so worried for her.
mad maddie:	**worrying won't do anything. it'll only stress u out.**
zoegirl:	yeah, but *not* worrying about it is like . . . denial. i mean, there's a very real chance that she'll have to move.
mad maddie:	**and there's an even realer chance that she won't. stop being a negative nelly.**

Send   Cancel

mad maddie:	and now the googlewhack attempt of the day. let's c, how about "graham's hero" . . .
zoegirl:	ur changing the subject!
mad maddie:	i'm sorry to report that graham's hero got 33,200 hits. guess ur not as special as u thought u were, zo.
zoegirl:	maddie, this is what denial *is*! doing every thing u can to deny that something's happening!
mad maddie:	no, this is called having fun on the computer searching for the perfect 1.
mad maddie:	i know, i'll try "sudsy canoodle," in honor of chive.
mad maddie:	2 hits! damn!
zoegirl:	only 2 hits, as compared to 33,200? isn't that good?
mad maddie:	2 was good when i first started. now it's just a taunt!

Thursday, November 25, 2:45 PM E.S.T.

SnowAngel:	hey, mads. i'm using one of those airport internet stations. it's a total rip-off, but i needed to escape my family.
mad maddie:	hey, girl! i'm so glad to hear from u! when does your plane take off?
SnowAngel:	2 soon, that's all i know. let's talk about something else. let's talk about the party.
mad maddie:	i'm totally with u.
mad maddie:	what'd u think of chive?
SnowAngel:	oh, he's CUTE, maddie! he's thoroughly cute, in a stoner boy kinda way.

mad maddie:	**chive is SO not a stoner boy. u just think that cuz he likes to party.**
SnowAngel:	no, i think that cuz of the way he acts, cuz of the way he looks at u all lazy and slow and appreciative. u know, like, "it's cool, dude." that's his vibe.
mad maddie:	**that's his VIBE?**
SnowAngel:	u know who he reminds me of? Matthew McConnaughey, with that sexy smile of his.
mad maddie:	**i'll take that. matthew m. is hot.**
mad maddie:	**and i'm very impressed u can spell his name.**
SnowAngel:	it's cuz i read "People"
mad maddie:	**but chive is so much more than "it's cool, dude." he's really into philosophy, and he's taking all these literature classes. didn't u hear him quoting charles bukowski while dylan funneled a beer?**
SnowAngel:	who's charles bukowski?
mad maddie:	**and that whole story about his dog, napoleon, and how he's gonna pimp him out by putting a gold chain around his neck. that cracked me up.**
SnowAngel:	i liked the fact that he went to the keg and got u refills. that was very gentlemanly.
mad maddie:	**a few 2 many refills, unfortunately**
SnowAngel:	well i wasn't gonna say anything . . .
mad maddie:	**i was so wasted i fell off the toilet seat. it was hysterical.**
SnowAngel:	yes, it sounds hysterical *looks extremely suspiciously at friend*
mad maddie:	**oh, don't go all zoe on me. i didn't tell her about that little incident, btw.**

Send   Cancel

41

SnowAngel:	fine, but i DO worry about u. just a little.
mad maddie:	**u don't need to. sometimes i get kinda psycho, but it's all fun and games.**
mad maddie:	**so were u surprised to c doug?**
SnowAngel:	that was so awesome that he came! i'm so proud of zoe for inviting him.
SnowAngel:	and for the record, she looked adorable in her embroidered jeans and that soft white shirt that actually shows off the fact she's a girl. i was like, "wow, did she dress up for the party?"
mad maddie:	**nah, not our zo. anyway, she came straight from work.**
SnowAngel:	with doug. i know. i made a point of talking to him, cuz he seemed so shell-shocked at being at a real live party.
mad maddie:	**oh no, teenagers on the loose! oh no, underage drinking!**
SnowAngel:	do u think he seemed different somehow? last nite he kinda seemed cuter to me than usual.
mad maddie:	**u r so funny. u just think that cuz for the 1st time in recorded history, he wasn't slobbering all over u. all of a sudden he's unattainable, so u miraculously think he's cute.**
SnowAngel:	unattainable? who says he's unattainable?
SnowAngel:	not that i WANT to attain him . . .
mad maddie:	**no, u just want him to lust after u in a constant state of angela-worship, like he did all last year. admit it!**
SnowAngel:	maybe he's gotten taller. maybe that's what it is.
SnowAngel:	anyway, i kinda ended up flirting with him a bit 2 much—i don't even know why. but that's ok, i'm sure he'd rather be flirted with than not flirted with.

Send   Cancel

mad maddie:	**a pity flirt. u r 2 kind.**
SnowAngel:	aren't i? i should give lessons to zoe. when i interrupted the 2 of them, she just stood there like a doormat. i was like, "liven up, zo! ur never gonna catch a guy like that!"
mad maddie:	**from where i stood, i'd say zoe was doing just fine.**
SnowAngel:	with DOUG? ☺
SnowAngel:	they're just friends. anyway, u were drunk
mad maddie:	**ugh, don't remind me**
SnowAngel:	crudballs, they're starting to board the plane.
mad maddie:	**wait, don't go!**
SnowAngel:	i have to, i have no choice
mad maddie:	**well call me from california— i want to hear how everything goes.**
SnowAngel:	i'll try, but my battery's low and i forgot my stupid charger.
SnowAngel:	real quick—did u like my "believe" bracelet?
mad maddie:	**i did, oddly enuff. i liked it very much.**
SnowAngel:	i keep touching it and looking down to admire it. i know it's stupid, but it gives me strength.
mad maddie:	**power to the bracelet! all bow down and chant "believe"!**

Thursday, November 25, 7:06 PM E.S.T.

| mad maddie: | **hey, zo. we came, we saw, we ate, and now i'm at java joe's escaping the hell hole that is my house. i snagged the only open computer, and a guy with a goatee is sending me** |

Send   Cancel

43

	death looks. can i help it if he wasn't smart enuff to put his stuff down BEFORE ordering his energy drink?
zoegirl:	u'd think he'd be 2 full for an energy drink. i can't even *imagine* putting an energy drink in my body. i am so stuffed!
mad maddie:	**well, tofu logs probably don't fill u up as much, and goatee-boy definitely looks like a tofu log kind of guy.**
zoegirl:	why is your house a hell hole?
mad maddie:	**cuz the moms is on her third glass of chardonnay, and the dishes are stacked to the ceiling. my brother's girlfriend has taken it upon herself to wash them, only she insists on doing it au naturel cuz it's better for the environment. she sent me out for dish soap—that's what i'm supposedly doing.**
zoegirl:	mark's still going strong with pelt-woman, huh?
zoegirl:	omg. i just realized something horrible. we've been calling her pelt-woman for so long that i can't remember her real name!
mad maddie:	**her armpit hair is long enuff to braid, zoe. her name IS pelt-woman.**
mad maddie:	**hey, have u talked to angela by any chance?**
zoegirl:	i did, but not for long cuz her phone died. but the short version is that she's not having fun.
mad maddie:	**well that's the surprise of the century.**
mad maddie:	**holidays suck. there's so much pressure.**
zoegirl:	i like holidays
mad maddie:	**that's cuz ur zoe and u've got the perfect family. that's cuz your mom and dad aren't gonna end up throwing beer cans at each other.**

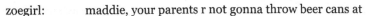

zoegirl:	maddie, your parents r not gonna throw beer cans at each other.
zoegirl:	r they?
mad maddie:	**fine, wine bottles. and chumley the psycho kitty will attack the remains of the turkey, and before the nite is over, pelt-woman will insist that we write something in her gratitude journal. and i will write, "i am grateful that the moms' empty chardonnay bottle only dislocated my shoulder and not my brain."**
zoegirl:	u r so full of it
zoegirl:	who's chumley the psycho kitty?
mad maddie:	**don't ask**
zoegirl:	i just did
mad maddie:	**oh. right.**
mad maddie:	**chumley is mark and pelt-woman's new cat. he's living with us until mark finds a place of his own.**
zoegirl:	and when will that be?
mad maddie:	**never, cuz he's a loser. he's 22 yrs old and the moms still tucks him in at nite.**
zoegirl:	lol
mad maddie:	**and ppl wonder why i have issues? exhibit a: my family.**
zoegirl:	aw, mads, *we're* your real family. me and angela.
mad maddie:	**believe me, i'd much rather be giving thanx with u guys. last year at this time, we were all sleeping under the stars on cumberland island. man, that was awesome.**
zoegirl:	hold on. *i* was sleeping under the stars, and i froze my butt off. *u* were hogging the tent.
mad maddie:	**the stars were pretty, tho. admit it.**

Send   Cancel

mad maddie:	uh oh, goatee boy is hovering behind me. he's saying, "um, excuse me, but the sign says 'for paying customers only'?"
zoegirl:	is he reading what ur writing?
mad maddie:	hell if i care. r u, goatee boy? r u reading what i'm writing?
mad maddie:	HA. he's pretending not to, but i can c from over my shoulder that he is. he looks all pinched and constipated.
zoegirl:	i have noticed that guys with goatees often look pinched and constipated. it's cuz they're trying so hard to be cool.
mad maddie:	it's cuz of 2 many tofu logs.
mad maddie:	alas, i must away to the grocery store. the dish soap is calling my name.
zoegirl:	goatee boy will be so happy
mad maddie:	nah, i'm turning the computer over to a girl on my other side. she has been waiting very patiently. she gets five gold stars!

Friday, November 26, 11:00 AM P.S.T.

SnowAngel:	hey, zo. i'm IMing from our crudballs hotel. i found an "office center" that has internet access, altho it's super slow.
zoegirl:	angela, hi!!! how r u? r u doing ok?
SnowAngel:	NO
SnowAngel:	i'm gonna tell u why, but i want maddie on-line 2. do u c the chatroom invite?
zoegirl:	got it!

Send   Cancel

46

lauren myracle

You have just entered the room "Angela's Boudoir."
mad maddie has entered the room.
zoegirl has entered the room.

zoegirl:	hi, mads!
mad maddie:	**hola, zo. so angela, what's the big news? did u convince your dad that california sucks?**
SnowAngel:	yeah, right. my dad doesn't CARE what i think.
SnowAngel:	guys . . . he took the job! he's starting in december!!!
mad maddie:	**WHAT?**
SnowAngel:	we're moving to california. we're frickin moving to california!
zoegirl:	omg, angela. in december???
SnowAngel:	dad's leaving in december. the rest of us r staying in atlanta until our house gets sold.
SnowAngel:	after that, we're gone!
mad maddie:	**nooooo, u can't move! u belong here with us!**
SnowAngel:	u think i don't know that?
SnowAngel:	and to add to the suckiness, my dad's boss has an awful daughter WHOM I DETEST. her name's glendy, if that doesn't say enuff!
mad maddie:	**glendy? sounds like a brand of toilet paper.**
SnowAngel:	she IS a brand of toilet paper. she's horrible.
zoegirl:	when did u meet her?
SnowAngel:	last nite, cuz we ended up having thanksgiving dinner at mr. boss's house instead of the hotel restaurant. aren't i lucky?
SnowAngel:	glendy was a freak, all big-eyed and blinky and

	burble-laffing every time i said anything, which was ridiculous cuz believe me i wasn't being remotely funny. she acts as if she's been homeschooled.
mad maddie:	**how old is she?**
SnowAngel:	she's 16 like us—not that u'd guess it cuz she's CLUELESS. she wanted to know where i got my glitter eyeshadow, and i was like, "at the store, u idiot." i was like, "don't u know your dad is an evil selfish pig? don't u know he's stealing my life away?"
zoegirl:	oh, poor angela!
SnowAngel:	and later she was all, "after u move here, we can have sleep-overs! we can give each other beauty treatments!!!" *slits wrists*
mad maddie:	**so when r u coming back?**
SnowAngel:	sunday. i can't wait. my mom thinks i'm being a brat cuz i'm not "appreciating this rare chance to c california," but i could care less. ☹
SnowAngel:	she's all, "consider this an opportunity," but i don't want an opportunity! i just wanna be with u guys!!!
zoegirl:	ok, so ur coming back on sunday . . . and then what?
SnowAngel:	the 4 of us r flying back to atlanta together, and then dad's gonna pack his stuff and fly out again in a week. mr. boss is gonna find him a place, and then who knows?
SnowAngel:	oh great—chrissy's here. stupid mom sent her down to get me, cuz we get to go sightseeing today with mr. boss and his fam. *holds dagger over heart*
mad maddie:	**shit, angela. i'm so sorry.**
zoegirl:	me 2

Send   Cancel

SnowAngel: me 3!!!

Saturday, November 27, 10:38 AM E.S.T.

zoegirl: hey, mads. i can't believe it—angela is actually moving! i hoped i'd wake up this morning and realize it was all a big mistake . . . but i didn't.

mad maddie: maybe her dad will change his mind. maybe he'll come to his senses.

zoegirl: i don't think so, maddie.

zoegirl: god, i miss her already, and she's not even officially gone.

mad maddie: zoe, don't

mad maddie: just . . . don't.

zoegirl: i thought maybe u'd wanna talk about it, that's all.

zoegirl: guess i was wrong.

Sunday, November 28, 4:05 PM E.S.T.

mad maddie: hi, zo. i'm bored.

zoegirl: me 2

mad maddie: wanna go meet angela at the airport?

zoegirl: omigod, what a great idea. she'd be so surprised!

zoegirl: only we can't. u can't go thru security unless ur a ticketed passenger.

mad maddie: we could wait at the welcome area. wanna? we could bring flowers and candy and a balloon shaped like a unicorn.

zoegirl: aw, mads, don't *ever* tell me ur not a big sap at heart.

Send   Cancel

zoegirl:	but yeah! let's do it!!!

Monday, November 29, 5:15 PM E.S.T.

SnowAngel:	k, it's official. my mother is driving me crazy. ever since we got back, she's been in a cleaning frenzy. i caught her trying to throw out a whole bag of old toys, including my complete set of My Pretty Ponies (!!!!), and all she said was, "this house is a junk heap. if i could, i'd throw it ALL away!"
mad maddie:	**even your beautiful Barbie balloon, given to u by your two bestest buds?**
SnowAngel:	well, no, not that. she thought that was very sweet, as did i.
SnowAngel:	but maddie? why did u give me a Barbie balloon?
mad maddie:	**cuz the gift store was out of unicorns. anywayz, zoe said u always wanted a Barbie named after u.**
mad maddie:	**is your mom making u get rid of your Barbies, too?**
SnowAngel:	yes. AND my pound puppies.
mad maddie:	**i loved those pound puppies**
SnowAngel:	me 2, except for the 1 with the crusty ear from when chrissy threw up on it. that one i didn't mind throwing away.
mad maddie:	**wait a sec, a.**
SnowAngel:	yes?
mad maddie:	**something has just occurred to me, and now i'm a little disturbed. u and zoe and i started hanging out in the 7th grade . . . why were u still playing with Barbies and pound puppies?**

50

Send   Cancel

SnowAngel: why were U? ur the 1 who just admitted to missing them!

mad maddie: hmm, ya got me there

mad maddie: not the Barbies, tho. i could give a rat's ass about Barbie—except when she's big and shiny and made of mylar.

SnowAngel: aaargh. i HATE cleaning. i would actually rather be back at school than at home right now. how sad is that?

mad maddie: ugh, not me. every single teacher was like, "now that we've returned from thanksgiving vacation, it's time to knuckle down. only 2 more weeks until final exams!"

SnowAngel: noooo, i can't handle it! 2 much pressure! *rips hair from head in clumps*

mad maddie: u need a glass of nestle quik to calm u down. have u ever noticed with nestle quik how u can actually crunch the chocolatey part? u swish a sip around in your mouth, and the chocolatey crystals just beg to be crunched. it's like at the dentist's, when he says, "ok, now lightly tap your teeth together for me." it's the exact same motion.

SnowAngel: oh great, mom's name just popped up on my buddy list. she's IMing me from downstairs. hold on while i c what she wants.

mad maddie: crunch, crunch, crunch. crunch, crunch, crunch. i'm singing a little song that goes crunch, crunch, crunch.

SnowAngel: i'm back—sorry about that.

mad maddie: what'd your mom say?

SnowAngel: she's such a dweeb. she's like, "hey, sweetie. i know this is stressful, but u've got to remember that it's

Send   Cancel

	stressful for all of us. i won't throw away any more of your junk, i promise. love ya, precious!"
mad maddie:	**that's so funny that she IMs u**
SnowAngel:	i know
mad maddie:	**it's not a bad idea, tho. hey, maybe i should suggest it to my parents. if they IMed each other, maybe they wouldn't yell so much.**
SnowAngel:	i don't wanna be here. come rescue me.
mad maddie:	**where do u wanna go?**
SnowAngel:	i don't care. just come get me!

Monday, November 29, 9:33 PM E.S.T.

SnowAngel:	hey, zo-ster. i saw u talking to doug today. r u guys becoming better friends?
zoegirl:	i guess so, yeah
zoegirl:	at work on saturday, this 1 little girl kept hugging him and telling him she loved him. it was so cute.
SnowAngel:	doug IS pretty lovable, i must admit. sometimes i think, "why in the world don't i just decide to like him?" in some ways it would be so easy—and i just know he'd make the perfect boyfriend.
zoegirl:	except i don't think u just "decide" things like that.
zoegirl:	anyway, there's the small and horrible fact that ur moving to california . . .
SnowAngel:	but maybe if i had a boyfriend, that would make it better. like, he could pine for me and send me flowers.

Send   Cancel

zoegirl:	*i'll* pine for u, angela. i'll pine for u like crazy!
SnowAngel:	i know, i know. just . . .
zoegirl:	just what?
SnowAngel:	well, u pining for me is good. i thoroughly expect absurd amounts of pining. but do me a favor and don't pine for anyone else, ok?
zoegirl:	huh?
SnowAngel:	doug, i mean. as in u and doug.
zoegirl:	ur telling me not to pine for doug???
zoegirl:	where in the world did *this* come from?
SnowAngel:	omg, it's insane, isn't it? it's just that i saw the way he was looking at u in the hall today, and i got this very weird feeling about it.
zoegirl:	what do u mean, the way he was looking at me? do u think maybe he
zoegirl:	never mind
SnowAngel:	oh, zoe, forget i said anything. i'm just fragile cuz of everything that's going on with me. it's like, i can't handle any more rejection!
zoegirl:	but angela, u've never been the slightest bit interested in doug. anyway, u had your chance with him last year.
SnowAngel:	but he wasn't as cute back then
zoegirl:	anyway, even if i *did* like doug—not that i do, cuz like u said that's insane—but why would that = rejection?
SnowAngel:	like i said, forget it
SnowAngel:	i'm gonna sign off before i say anything else stupid. bye!

Send   Cancel   53

Tuesday, November 30, 10:18 PM E.S.T.

SnowAngel: maddie, a realtor came to our house today.

mad maddie: oh god. what'd she say?

SnowAngel: that our house is lovely. i hate her.

SnowAngel: she's gonna send over a "stager" to put in fake plants and stuff, and we're supposed to pop popcorn before any showings so that the house will smell buttery.

mad maddie: man, that's nuts

SnowAngel: she also said that altho sales are usually slow in the winter, there's a small peak in december. i wanted to stab her eyeballs.

mad maddie: well . . . maybe there won't be a peak in december. try not to think about it.

SnowAngel: maddie, my dad flies out TOMORROW. how am i supposed to not think about it?

SnowAngel: i'm so furious at him, but at the same time i don't want him to leave.

mad maddie: he is a very bad man. i'm furious at him 2.

SnowAngel: i'm exhausted. call my cell, will ya? i wanna keep talking, but i wanna lie down.

mad maddie: ok

SnowAngel: bye! call me!!!

Wednesday, December 1, 4:33 PM E.S.T.

SnowAngel: my dad's officially in california. tonite he'll sleep in the new apartment, and tomorrow he'll wake up and

54

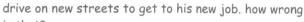

	drive on new streets to get to his new job. how wrong is that?
zoegirl:	i'm so sorry, angela. i know how u must feel.
SnowAngel:	no u don't. u would never be in this situation, cuz your dad's, like, the CEO of his company. he's the 1 who would be doing the firing, not the 1 who would ever get fired.
zoegirl:	well, he *could* get fired if the stockholders voted him out.
SnowAngel:	yeah, fat chance
zoegirl:	angela . . . what's going on? do u *want* my dad to get fired?
SnowAngel:	aaargh *bonks head on desk*
SnowAngel:	no, i don't want your dad to get fired. but i don't wanna move, either. i told mom that i'd rather live in a box outside the mall. i told her i wanna stay here and live with my aunt sadie.
zoegirl:	that's a brilliant idea! could u do that, for real?
SnowAngel:	mom wouldn't even consider it. she was just, "angela, don't be silly."
zoegirl:	that sucks
SnowAngel:	i know, especially since aunt sadie's the only person in my family who's been the least bit supportive thru all this. i talked to her tonite, and she was like, "don't tell your mom, but i think it's 2 bad jeff took that job without even considering other options. a girl shouldn't be uprooted from her friends during her junior yr of high school."
zoegirl:	so so so so true

ttfn

SnowAngel:	yeah
SnowAngel:	that's all i wanted to say, really. bye.

Thursday, December 2, 7:17 PM E.S.T.

SnowAngel:	maddie, i've got something terrible to confess. i went shopping today cuz i was super depressed, and—er—i seem to have bought a shirt-on-shirt. please don't hate me!
mad maddie:	**huh?**
SnowAngel:	it's sooooo tacky, i know. *ducks for cover*
mad maddie:	**what, pray tell, is a shirt-on-shirt?**
SnowAngel:	it's . . . u know, a long sleeve shirt with a short sleeve shirt on top of it, only the long sleeve shirt is a fakeout, cuz except for the sleeves and collar it doesn't really exist. it's the layered look, so i can look slouchy-cool w/o half-trying.
mad maddie:	**oh, angela, no.**
SnowAngel:	but it's really really cute! the long sleeve part is white and the short sleeve part is baby blue to match my eyes.
mad maddie:	**next thing u know, ur gonna be buying fake vintage t-shirts from old navy. ppl will say, "ooo, where'd u get that great shirt? have u really been to bob's hawaiian luau?" and u'll blush and stammer and say, "uh, no, i found it at a thrift store," which will be such a lie! UR LIVING A LIE, ANGELA SILVER!!!**
SnowAngel:	well it's my aunt sadie's fault, cuz she's the 1 who

	whisked me off to the mall. she said i needed some good old-fashioned girl time.
mad maddie:	**that's nice, i suppose. altho a little unnerving that your aunt sadie considers herself a "girl."**
SnowAngel:	as opposed to what, a man?
mad maddie:	**as opposed to a WOMAN. as in, a grown-up adult-acting person our parents' age. not that u'd know it to look at her.**
SnowAngel:	i know—isn't she adorable? she shops in Gap Kids cuz the jeans there r cheaper, and she's tiny enuff that she can get away with it. i wanna be just like her when i grow up.
mad maddie:	**or when u fail to grow up, as the case may be. lemme guess: your aunt played hooky from work to take u shopping. did i nail it?**
SnowAngel:	maybe
mad maddie:	**and did she have all sorts of funky barrettes jammed in her hair? and was she wearing her hipster shoes with the mile-high platforms?**
SnowAngel:	so? what would u recommend—turning all matronly and wearing rubber-soled orthopedic loafers? *shudders*
mad maddie:	**i'm just giving u a hard time. u know i think your aunt sadie is cool.**
SnowAngel:	we had so much fun at Claire's Boutique, trying on all the tacky jewelry. i bought a sparkly dragonfly pin to go with my shirt-on-shirt.
mad maddie:	**well, aren't u clever**
SnowAngel:	why, yes i am

Send   Cancel   57

ttfn

SnowAngel:	hey, "the OC" starts in 15 minutes. wanna come watch?
mad maddie:	**oh, that reminds me. chive posted something funny about the OC on his blog. hold on and i'll copy it so u can c . . .**
SnowAngel:	chive has a blog?
mad maddie:	**a deadjournal, yeah**
SnowAngel:	what's a deadjournal?
mad maddie:	**it's like a livejournal, only better. instead of having "friends," u have "fiends," and your blog's called your grave. the whole site is called the cemetery.**
SnowAngel:	sounds goth 😕
mad maddie:	**nah, just anti-establishment**
mad maddie:	**here's his post from last week:**

> **Hey, I know. Let's take a group of twenty-something actors and let them relive their glory days. Surfers pretending to be emo kids, rich kids pretending to have issues, Chino Boy pretending to have soul. Oh, and don't forget, let's insert some previously good indie bands who ACTUALLY HAVE TALENT, and let's throw so much money at them that they're forced to sell out, performing in front of scenesters pretending to be teenagers pretending to be real.**
>
> **Oh well. At least there's good tunes!**

SnowAngel:	what?! "the OC" is one of the few good and true things in this world, i'll have u know.

Send   Cancel

SnowAngel:	anyway, how does chive know so much about it if he doesn't watch it, huh?
mad maddie:	**i know, that's what's so funny. chive LOVES the OC—he just rags on it for the hell of it. in fact he thinks u should move to orange county instead of el cerrito.**
SnowAngel:	well, duh, so do i
SnowAngel:	hey, i know! i'll run away and live in the cohens' pool house with ryan!
mad maddie:	**u, run away? and be separated from your straightening iron?**
SnowAngel:	i could stash my straightening iron in my backpack. public bathrooms have electrical outlets, u know.
mad maddie:	**no they don't**
SnowAngel:	yes they do
mad maddie:	**no, angela, they don't. trust me.**
SnowAngel:	well . . . then i'd find a library and do my hair there. there are definitely outlets in libraries, cuz i've seen people bring their computers and tap away.
mad maddie:	**i can c it now. to the right are the studious computer folk, working hard on their papers, and to the left is angela, plunked down on the floor and straightening her hair.**
SnowAngel:	and the problem is . . . ?
mad maddie:	**sorry, darlin, u wouldn't last a minute as a runaway.**
SnowAngel:	*sticks out tongue*
SnowAngel:	so r u gonna come watch with me or not?
mad maddie:	**i can't—i already said i'd watch it with chive. we're gonna down a shot every time seth looks longingly at summer. wanna join?**

Send   Cancel

SnowAngel:	no thank u. ur defiling the OC experience, u very bad girl.
mad maddie:	**know what else chive loves, and what we'll probably watch after the OC?**
mad maddie:	**"Full House"**
SnowAngel:	WITH THE OLSEN TWINS? CHIVE HAS A THING FOR THE OLSEN TWINS???
mad maddie:	**for that one, we drink every time that obnoxious kid kimmy shows up.**
SnowAngel:	maddie, Full House doesn't come on after the OC whatcha gonna do about that, huh?
mad maddie:	**tivo, baby, tivo!**

Friday, December 3, 4:15 PM E.S.T.

zoegirl:	hey, mads. i'm at my mom's office, sitting in the most phenomenal swivel chair ever invented. can i have a swivel chair like this when i grow up?
mad maddie:	**depends. r u gonna be a high-powered lawyer like your mom and make tons of money?**
zoegirl:	uh . . .
mad maddie:	**i, for one, plan to reject all worldly objects. u can come visit me in my trailer if you want. i will have christmas lights blinking all year long.**
mad maddie:	**so wazzup?**
zoegirl:	have u ever heard of
zoegirl:	ok, this is embarrassing. i don't know how to say it. but have u ever heard of girls, like, pleasuring themselves by jiggling their legs?

mad maddie:	**WHAT?!!**
mad maddie:	**omg, i am rolling on the floor, just so you know. just exactly how phenomenal IS that swivel chair?**
zoegirl:	maddie! not *me*! god!
mad maddie:	**and the term is "masturbating," zoe. u can say it. mas-tur-bat-ing.**
zoegirl:	fyi, i don't do that. sometimes i wish i could, but i can't, so that's that.
mad maddie:	**what do u mean, u can't?**
zoegirl:	i can't, that's all
mad maddie:	**r u serious?**
zoegirl:	this is not actually what i IMed to talk about. but yes, i'm serious.
zoegirl:	can u?
mad maddie:	**can i MASTURBATE?**
mad maddie:	**uh, zoe, where is your mom? she's not in the room with u, is she?**
zoegirl:	yeah, she's standing right behind me, maddie.
zoegirl:	she's in a meeting, u doof! i've been waiting here *forever* cuz we're meeting my dad for dinner.
mad maddie:	**well in that case . . . yes, i can pleasure myself quite nicely, thank u very much. and i'm only telling u that cuz ur one of my dearest friends on the planet. but don't go asking for lessons.**
zoegirl:	oh, gross!
mad maddie:	**r u gonna explain what brought this up in the first place? what's this "jiggling their legs" business?**
zoegirl:	grrrrrrrrrrr

Send	Cancel	

zoegirl:	chase dickinson, during french. he looked over at me and started cracking up, and i was like, "what? what r u laffing about?" he jerked his chin at my legs, which happened to be crossed, and said, "i know why girls do that." "do *what*?" i said. "jiggle your leg like that."
mad maddie:	**WERE u jiggling your leg?**
zoegirl:	i might have been. so? i wasn't doing . . . what he said i was doing!
mad maddie:	**don't let it bother u. he's an immature freak.**
zoegirl:	i couldn't have been doing that even if i wanted to, not that i *ever* would have been doing it right there in french. i mean, god. but sometimes i think there's something wrong with me, maddie. why doesn't my body work the way other ppl's do?
mad maddie:	**hmm, cuz ur repressed?**
mad maddie:	**uh oh, ur not responding**
mad maddie:	**i was KIDDING, zoe!**
zoegirl:	that was not a nice thing to say
mad maddie:	**i'm sorry, i'm sorry. i was just teasing.**
zoegirl:	i don't wanna be repressed. i just think . . . i dunno. that some girls r more naturally sexual than others. like u.
mad maddie:	**chive told me i'm sexy. he said i have great legs.**
zoegirl:	u do have great legs. u have great everything.
zoegirl:	r u *sure* the 2 of u aren't becoming an item? angela said u watched "the OC" with him last nite.
mad maddie:	**yeah, and i totally made a fool of myself. not during the show, but after.**
zoegirl:	uh oh. what happened?

Send   Cancel

mad maddie:	1 of chive's friends from northside was there, a girl named whitney, and she was all over chive. it was disgusting. and i guess i was a little . . .
mad maddie:	i dunno. but somehow i ended up getting paired off with this guy named brannen, who also goes to n'side.
zoegirl:	what do u mean, paired off?
mad maddie:	the 4 of us were out by the pool, which was closed, but we climbed over the fence. and whitney was like, "i'll kiss chive, and u kiss brannen, ok?"
zoegirl:	she calls him "chive" too?
mad maddie:	everybody does now. i love that.
zoegirl:	if ur the one who came up his nickname, and ur the one who likes him, then *u* should get to kiss him.
mad maddie:	i know. i think so 2. but whitney had already claimed him, so what was i supposed to do?
mad maddie:	anywayz, who cares? bodies r bodies r bodies.
zoegirl:	no, cuz bodies r connected to actual people, to hearts and brains and souls.
zoegirl:	was brannen cute at least?
mad maddie:	ehhh, 2 short for my taste. and u know what's bad?
zoegirl:	what?
mad maddie:	it turned into this total horndog macking session, with my bra shoved up and his hands all over me, and now he won't quit IMing. he's like, "do u wanna go to a movie? do u wanna go out for coffee?"
mad maddie:	i finally wrote back and said, "enuff, all rite? quit feeling sorry for me."
zoegirl:	i doubt he feels sorry for u, mads

Send   Cancel

mad maddie:	**that's what HE said. he's all, "what? no, i really like u!"**
mad maddie:	**whatevs**
zoegirl:	i don't get it. u and chive have so much fun together, and it's obvious he's attracted to u or he wouldn't have kissed u at donovan's wedding. so why would he kiss whitney instead of u?
mad maddie:	**cuz she basically told him 2. it's not like he was gonna tell her no.**
zoegirl:	i don't c why not
mad maddie:	**plus she's pretty, in a bouncy cheerleader-y way.**
zoegirl:	did he even seem apologetic about it?
mad maddie:	**it wasn't a big deal, zo. i refuse to be a ball and chain.**
zoegirl:	omg
mad maddie:	**anywayz, i'm gonna c him later on tonite. he says he's got something planned, but he won't tell me what.**
zoegirl:	is whitney gonna be there?
zoegirl:	this is making me not like chive as much, that he would treat u like this.
mad maddie:	**like what? i'm a big girl—i can make my own decisions.**
mad maddie:	**i can't even blame whitney for liking him. he's just got that kind of energy, where everyone wants to be around him. he makes everyone feel special.**
zoegirl:	not special enuff, apparently . . .
mad maddie:	**i'm so glad u know everything about relationships, zo. i'm so glad ur such a pure and shining example of how to do things right.**
zoegirl:	haha
zoegirl:	if it makes u feel any better, i kinda have boy probs of my own.

64

mad maddie:	**oh, how lovely. please elaborate.**
zoegirl:	well . . . but u *can't* tell angela. anyway, it'll probably come to nothing.
mad maddie:	**what'll come to nothing?**
mad maddie:	**OMG—is it about u and doug?**
zoegirl:	what?!! how did u know?
mad maddie:	**it just came to me in a flash, cuz why else would u be all interested in this leg-jiggling business?**
zoegirl:	maddie!
zoegirl:	never mind, i'm not dignifying that with a response.
mad maddie:	**so u WERE flirting with him at dylan's. i knew it! zoe likes doug! zoe likes doug!**
zoegirl:	shut up!
mad maddie:	**omg, if angela finds out she's gonna FREAK.**
zoegirl:	i know, but why? it's totally unfair for her to even care. yes, he had a crush on her last year, but now they're just friends.
mad maddie:	**does angela know that?**
zoegirl:	of course she knows that. she's the one who never reciprocated. how would she think they're anything BUT friends?
mad maddie:	**cuz in angela's mind, doug is her safety date, the guy who'll long for her forever. and one day she could have a change of heart, and they would live sappily ever after.**
zoegirl:	that's not gonna happen, maddie
mad maddie:	**well no, not with U in the picture.**
mad maddie:	**u better tell her, zo**
zoegirl:	there's nothing to tell. i don't know why i even told u!

Send   Cancel

65

mad maddie:	**well u can't give me a hard time about chive, that's for sure. not when ur the 1 sneaking around behind angela's back.**
mad maddie:	**don't say i didn't warn u!**

Saturday, December 4, 11:09 AM E.S.T.

SnowAngel:	hi, mads. wake up wake up wake up!
mad maddie:	**ugh. 2 groggy. go away.**
SnowAngel:	then why r u on the computer, huh? gotcha there, sucker.
mad maddie:	**can't talk. downloading a song from a group chive told me about. go away.**
SnowAngel:	i'm not going away.
SnowAngel:	so how was your nite? *folds hands and waits with a pleasant smile*
mad maddie:	**u really wanna know?**
SnowAngel:	yes, i really wanna know.
mad maddie:	**well, u can't flip out, but i'll tell u cuz ur my friend.**
SnowAngel:	hmm, intrigue. i luv it.
mad maddie:	**i smoked pot for the first time, ok?**
SnowAngel:	WHAT???
mad maddie:	**it was SO not a big deal. chive said he had a surprise for me, and that's what it was.**
SnowAngel:	chive's surprise was that the 2 of u were gonna smoke pot?!
mad maddie:	**and his friend brannen, which was a mistake. not the fact that i smoked pot, but the fact that brannen was there 2.**

Send   Cancel

SnowAngel:	brannen from the OC nite?
mad maddie:	**if i'd known he was gonna be there, i might not have gone. cuz the pot, like, intensified everything, and partly that was cool, but partly it was uncool, especially in regards to brannen.**
SnowAngel:	why?
mad maddie:	**i dunno, cuz he kept staring at me with this "i'm interested in u" smile. it was gross.**
SnowAngel:	what about chive?
mad maddie:	**he was in his own world listening to his iPod. i wish i could be more like that, just do whatever i feel like doing and be confident in myself. but no. i had to deal with brannen making pop-eyes at me.**
SnowAngel:	where were u guys this whole time?
mad maddie:	**we sneaked into a housing development called cross creek condominiums. there's this big stretch of forest behind the condos, and that's where we went.**
SnowAngel:	oh
mad maddie:	**we called ourselves the cross creek crusaders. it was pretty funny.**
SnowAngel:	i can't believe u smoked pot. i mean, i know ppl do, but i can't believe that U did.
SnowAngel:	what was it like?
mad maddie:	**kinda a mixed bag**
mad maddie:	**ha, that's funny. a mixed BAG, get it?**
SnowAngel:	no
mad maddie:	**as in, a bag of pot. that's what u call it.**
SnowAngel:	fascinating. now tell me what it was like

mad maddie:	well, it hurt sucking it in. and then ur supposed to hold it for as long as u can, but i kept coughing. and it made my eyes water.
SnowAngel:	sounds fun. NOT!
mad maddie:	chive says i'll get better with practice. he says the paranoid feelings will go away, 2.
SnowAngel:	huh
SnowAngel:	um, i know this'll sound kinda stupid, but what's the GOOD part about smoking pot? besides the fact that it was something u did with chive.
mad maddie:	well . . . i seriously had some wild sensations. it made everything blurry around the edges, if that makes sense. like the boundaries of the world were melting away, and all these undercurrents of life were swirling around us. and i could SEE them, that's what made it so cool.
SnowAngel:	u could c what? the undercurrents of life?
mad maddie:	i know it sounds weird. i guess there's no way to explain it unless u've tried it yourself.
SnowAngel:	my life is blurry enuff, thanx
SnowAngel:	r u gonna do it again?
mad maddie:	i dunno. i wish it didn't burn so much.
mad maddie:	but chive mentioned something about hooking up tonite, so who knows. wanna come?
SnowAngel:	er . . . doesn't really seem like my scene.
mad maddie:	ur always saying u want to get to know chive better, and anywayz, zoe's working tonite so u have no excuse. u don't have to smoke if u don't want to.
SnowAngel:	i don't wanna sneak into that golf course place, either

Send   Cancel

mad maddie:	it's not a golf course! it's just the woods behind some condos.
mad maddie:	why don't i call chive and c what's up, and then i'll give u more details. we'll do something legal if that's what u want.
SnowAngel:	uh . . . ok, i guess
mad maddie:	hey, that just gave me a good idea for a googlewhack.
SnowAngel:	qu'est ce que c'est un googlewhack?
mad maddie:	i haven't told u about googlewhacks?
mad maddie:	oh yeah, that was zoe
SnowAngel:	*taps foot on floor*
mad maddie:	a googlewhack is an extremely delightful way to pass the time where u type in words on google and try to get only 1 hit. the "perfect 1," it's called.
SnowAngel:	sounds boring
SnowAngel:	or rather, sounds like something u should do ON YOUR OWN and not while your friend is twiddling away her toes.
mad maddie:	i'm gonna try "legal chive," whaddaya think? let me just open a new screen here . . .
mad maddie:	tarnation. 20,100 hits.
SnowAngel:	oh well, so much for that
mad maddie:	maybe "illegal chive" is the way to go, eh?
SnowAngel:	maddie, i do not wanna sit here while u googlewhack!
mad maddie:	716 hits. that's still pretty shabby. wouldn't it be funny if all 716 were actually about chive and his illegal activities?

Send   Cancel   69

SnowAngel:	wouldn't it be even funnier if u actually talked to ME instead of googlewhacking off in the corner?
mad maddie:	**ooo, u make me sound so perverted**
SnowAngel:	good-bye, i'm signing off
mad maddie:	**what? WHY?**
SnowAngel:	cuz ur making my eyes glaze over. anyway, i've gotta clean up my room for an open house today. UGH.
mad maddie:	**well, in that case maybe i'll go hunt down some breakfast—maybe some more of that pizza i had last nite. u know, pizza hut pizza is truly amazing. it's been in our fridge for 2 weeks, but it tastes as good as ever.**
SnowAngel:	did u say . . . 2 weeks? *goes pale*
mad maddie:	**i didn't even heat it up. mmm-mmm good!**

Saturday, December 4, 11:52 AM E.S.T.

SnowAngel:	omg, i just realized! chive IS a stoner!!!
mad maddie:	**huh?**
SnowAngel:	i said he was a stoner at dylan's party, and u were like, "nooooo." but he's TOTALLY a stoner-boy.
SnowAngel:	u knew it all along, didn't u?
mad maddie:	**well . . .**
mad maddie:	**he's way more than that, tho. he's not JUST a stoner-boy.**
SnowAngel:	i'm just saying. *looks knowingly at friend*
SnowAngel:	u can't pull 1 over on me, madderoo!

Sunday, December 5, 9:18 AM E.S.T.

SnowAngel:	mornin', sunshine. did u have fun at work last nite?
SnowAngel:	zoe?
SnowAngel:	wow, it must have been REALLY good if it's taking u this long to answer. either that or really bad . . .
zoegirl:	sorry, sorry, i was signing off with someone else
SnowAngel:	oh yeah? who?
zoegirl:	just someone
SnowAngel:	well now i'm curious. WHO?
zoegirl:	it was doug, that's all. he IMed me; i didn't IM him.
SnowAngel:	doug IMed u? why?
SnowAngel:	did he ask about me?
zoegirl:	u know, angela, it's not *always* about u.
zoegirl:	we were talking about work, that's all. about that little kid who cracks us up, graham cracker. last nite graham kept presenting his cheek to me and saying, "u can kiss me if u want. little boys need lots of kisses."
SnowAngel:	aww, i love little kids. they're so pure. 😊
SnowAngel:	wanna know what i did last nite? and just to give u a hint, "pure" would not be the way to describe it.
zoegirl:	that's right, u went out with maddie and chive, didn't u?
SnowAngel:	AND meade AND brannen AND whitney.
SnowAngel:	i have to tell u, zoe, i'm feeling kinda weird about it.
zoegirl:	how come?
SnowAngel:	i dunno, i've been trying to figure it out. i've been trying to figure out chive, mainly. maddie really likes him, u know.

Send   Cancel

zoegirl:	do u not?
SnowAngel:	no, i DO like him—at least when i'm around him. he's smart, even tho he talks so s-l-o-w-l-y. and he's funny. he was totally cracking me up last nite, calling everyone "boogie." as in, "m-boogie, what's happening?" or "c'mon over here, a-boogie, and get yo-self some chips."
zoegirl:	he *is* pretty charming, isn't he? i remember that from dylan's party.
SnowAngel:	AND he's extremely hot
SnowAngel:	i can c why maddie's ga-ga over him. i just think he holds 2 much power over her.
zoegirl:	like jana last year?
SnowAngel:	maybe . . . but different. chive isn't trying to use maddie, i don't think. and he DOES care about her, i can tell. he just doesn't care about her ENUFF.
zoegirl:	maybe he doesn't care about anyone enuff.
zoegirl:	u know he kissed whitney, right? but maddie was all, "it's no big deal, bodies r bodies, blah blah blah."
SnowAngel:	last nite chive was giving maddie all kinds of attention—laffing at her jokes, looking at her in that lazy, bemused way of his—but he was sitting next to whitney and stroking her forearm the whole time.
zoegirl:	ick. that is *so* uncool.
SnowAngel:	i'm sure maddie can't be 2 thrilled about that, but of course she won't admit it.
zoegirl:	i don't get it. there's no way i could watch the guy i like fool around with another girl.
SnowAngel:	"the guy u like"? who's the guy u like?

Send   Cancel

zoegirl:	what? nobody!
SnowAngel:	then why would u say that?
zoegirl:	why would i say what?
SnowAngel:	zoe, r u hiding something?
zoegirl:	angela, please. anyway, we're talking about chive, remember?
SnowAngel:	oh yeah
SnowAngel:	did u know he's a stoner? and that now maddie's becoming one 2?
zoegirl:	becoming a *stoner*?
zoegirl:	no way
SnowAngel:	she's tried it, tho. she really has.
zoegirl:	tried *pot*?
SnowAngel:	yes, pot. 🌿 weed, ganja, doobage, gank.
zoegirl:	gank? gank is an extremely stupid word.
zoegirl:	and no, i didn't know she tried it, cuz of course she didn't tell me.
SnowAngel:	cuz she thinks ur a nun 🙂
zoegirl:	that is so irritating. and she shouldn't be smoking pot. it kills brain cells. doesn't she know that?
SnowAngel:	i'm not even sure she liked it that much, from what she said.
zoegirl:	but i bet she pretends she does in front of chive. am i right? to protect her tough-girl image?
SnowAngel:	well . . . possibly. i was afraid they were gonna light up again last nite, but they didn't. brannen was like, "we're out of pot, dude. who's gonna go on a pot run?" but nobody ever did anything about it.

Send   Cancel

73

zoegirl:	lovely
SnowAngel:	crap, i g2g. my mom's yelling at me from downstairs—some family is here for a 2nd showing of the house.
zoegirl:	a 2nd showing? oh no!
SnowAngel:	don't worry, i have a plan. i heard the evil realtor say that the man wants to know about our neighbors, cuz his current neighbors r really loud. so as i leave, i'm gonna happen to mention the thoroughly bitchin' garage band that practices 2 doors down. *snickers*
zoegirl:	what garage band?
SnowAngel:	what do u mean, what garage band?
SnowAngel:	ttfn!

Monday, December 6, 10:15 PM E.S.T.

mad maddie:	**z-boogie! i saw u hanging out with doug at his locker, and unless i am mistaken (which i sincerely hope i am), i heard him saying something very disturbing.**
zoegirl:	what r u talking about?
mad maddie:	**ahem. and i quote, "u can kiss me if you want. little boys need lots of kisses." !!!**
zoegirl:	oh god. u heard that?
mad maddie:	**what kind of twisted games r u 2 playing, zo? PLEASE tell me u don't pretend to be his mommy. PLEASE tell me u don't spank his iddle-widdle bottom.**
zoegirl:	maddie, gross!!!
mad maddie:	**WELL?**

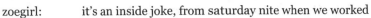

zoegirl:	it's an inside joke, from saturday nite when we worked together. he wasn't really being himself. he was just being . . . cute.
mad maddie:	**"little boys need lots of kisses"?!!!**
zoegirl:	*please* stop. ur making me blush.
mad maddie:	**have u told angela yet? cuz i gotta say, if ur gonna be flirting with him in the hall, she's gonna find out.**
zoegirl:	i know, i know . . . but there's so much going on with her right now. i don't wanna make things more complicated. and i don't wanna make her mad at me.
mad maddie:	**ha—i would love it if she got mad at u. she NEVER gets mad at u.**
zoegirl:	maddie, that's a terrible thing to say! why would u even say that?
mad maddie:	**that's why u have to TELL her, u idiot. on every single sitcom in the world, this is how problems start. some idiot plays dumb and doesn't tell someone else what's really going on, and then there's mass confusion and mistaken assumptions and everything ends in chaos. u should know this, zoe.**
zoegirl:	i *do* know. i do. but when ur in the middle of it—in real life, not tv—it's completely different. it's harder than u think to tell the truth.
mad maddie:	**not for me**
zoegirl:	then u tell her!
mad maddie:	**no ma'am, miss zoe. i'm having 2 much fun watching u squirm.**
zoegirl:	i can tell

Send Cancel

75

ttfn

mad maddie:	**i want u to swear to me right now that u'll straighten this whole mess out, mmmkay?**
zoegirl:	fine. i will, i really will.
mad maddie:	**when?**
zoegirl:	tomorrow, i promise
mad maddie:	**i'm doing this for your own good, u know!**

Tuesday, December 7, 9:09 AM E.S.T.

mad maddie:	**dude! u got my message!**
zoegirl:	phone's on vibrate, otherwise i wouldn't have.
mad maddie:	**ooo, vibrate. is it as good as your special chair?**
zoegirl:	what do u want now that u made me get on-line?
mad maddie:	**have u told angela about doug?**
zoegirl:	not yet
mad maddie:	**u better!**

Tuesday, December 7, 10:53 AM E.S.T.

mad maddie:	**have u told her?**
zoegirl:	stop IMing me on my phone!
mad maddie:	**so u haven't?**
zoegirl:	ms. aiken is staring. i'm logging off!

Tuesday, December 7, 1:48 PM E.S.T.

mad maddie:	**hi, zo. do u feel like ur being spied on?**

Send   Cancel

76

zoegirl:	maddie, what r u doing here? this isn't your free.
mad maddie:	**peaches doesn't care. she loves me. anywayz, the media center isn't your own private idaho.**
mad maddie:	**have u told angela?**
zoegirl:	no, cuz i'm being stalked by a deranged lunatic.
zoegirl:	plus, when would i have? i haven't gotten the chance.
mad maddie:	**what about lunch, u big fat liar? she was sitting 2 feet away from u.**
zoegirl:	i'll tell her as soon as i get home from school. r u satisfied? now go away. i have to finish this paper.
mad maddie:	**catch ya laters!**

Tuesday, December 7, 3:45 PM E.S.T.

mad maddie:	**ur home from school, obviously. HAVE U TOLD HER?**
zoegirl:	u r a freak. i'm calling her right now. bye!

Tuesday, December 7, 4:12 PM E.S.T.

zoegirl:	hi, maddie. it's me.
mad maddie:	**well?!!**
zoegirl:	i didn't tell her.
mad maddie:	**omg, ur pathetic. what's your excuse this time?**
zoegirl:	they sold the house, mads. her mom sold the house.
mad maddie:	**WHAT?!!!**
zoegirl:	they're moving as soon as finals r over!!!
mad maddie:	**as soon as**

Send   Cancel   77

mad maddie:	**zoe, that's less than 2 weeks!**
zoegirl:	i know
mad maddie:	**i just**
mad maddie:	**i don't even**
mad maddie:	**they're seriously moving? this is real?**
zoegirl:	angela could barely get the words out, she was crying so hard.
mad maddie:	**holy fucking shit**
mad maddie:	**where r they gonna LIVE?**
zoegirl:	the apartment mr. silver rented has 3 bedrooms, so they'll join him there. i guess that was the plan all along.
zoegirl:	what r we gonna do, maddie?
mad maddie:	**i have no flipping idea**
mad maddie:	**but for now, we better get going.**
zoegirl:	where, to angela's?
mad maddie:	**where else?!**

Thursday, December 9, 9:14 PM E.S.T.

zoegirl:	hey, mads. have u checked angela's profile today? it's so sad.
mad maddie:	**i know. i was gonna IM her, but then i saw the scowly face and i thought, "ooo, better back off."**
zoegirl:	i had the same thought, but then i realized that right now is when she needs us the most. so i called her—and she sounded *very* depressed.
mad maddie:	**well, duh. she's moving 3,000 miles away.**
zoegirl:	it was like she wasn't even angela anymore. her voice

Send   Cancel

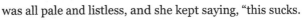

	was all pale and listless, and she kept saying, "this sucks. this just totally sucks."
mad maddie:	**that's how she was at lunch, 2**
zoegirl:	i tried in my nicest way to suggest that being depressed isn't gonna help anything, and she goes, "i think it's an appropriate response, zoe." like i was being stupid for trying to cheer her up.
mad maddie:	**we should do something fun tomorrow nite. maybe that would help.**
zoegirl:	yeah, sounds good. i feel bad that i can't do something with her tomorrow nite *and* saturday nite, but i've gotta work.
mad maddie:	**where u'll c doug, natch**
mad maddie:	**u still haven't told angela, have u?**
zoegirl:	it's so not the point right now. it would just make her feel worse.
mad maddie:	**ur playing with fire, zoe. mark my words, this is gonna come back and bite u on the ass!**

Friday, December 10, 4:44 PM E.S.T.

mad maddie:	**hey, gal. since u never decided what u wanna do tonite, zoe and i decided for u. put your party hat on . . . cuz we're going BOWLING!!!**
SnowAngel:	*lifts head from the depths of hell* bowling?
mad maddie:	**chop chop! if we get there early, we can beat the rush.**
SnowAngel:	there's a rush to go bowling?
mad maddie:	**on a friday nite? we're talking high drama, baby. ker-ash! she scores another strike!**

SnowAngel:	i haven't gone bowling since last year when i went with doug and steve and chrissy. doug and steve slipped notes into the holes in chrissy's ball and pretended they were from someone on the staff, remember?
SnowAngel:	that was so fun. but nothing will ever be fun again.
mad maddie:	**YES IT WILL. and btw, be sure to wear crappy shoes. don't ask—just do it.**
SnowAngel:	pardon me, but i don't own any crappy shoes
SnowAngel:	hey, do u think doug would come with us if we called him? maybe that's what i need to perk me up, a dose of doug-love.
mad maddie:	**er . . . no doug. this is a girls' nite, full of bonding and wacky hijinks.**
SnowAngel:	right, right
SnowAngel:	but i have been thinking . . . maybe, before i leave, i'll give doug something to remember me by. *wink, wink* he's certainly waited for it long enuff.
mad maddie:	**angela, no**
SnowAngel:	why? it would be the thrill of his life.
mad maddie:	**it's a bad idea. trust me.**
SnowAngel:	yeah, i guess it wouldn't be fair. *sigh*
mad maddie:	**that's right. leave the poor guy alone.**
SnowAngel:	altho who said love was fair? and long-distance relationships CAN work, u know . . .
mad maddie:	**FORGET ABOUT DOUG**
mad maddie:	**now listen. go dig thru your closet and find your rattiest sneaks. i'm coming to pick u up!**

Send   Cancel

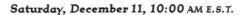

Saturday, December 11, 10:00 AM E.S.T.

SnowAngel:	morning, zo
zoegirl:	morning, angela. u wearing your bowling shoes?
SnowAngel:	at 10 in the morning? i'm in my bunny slippers, sweetheart.
SnowAngel:	but yeah, i've got them right here beside me. *pats hideous bowling shoes lovingly* i didn't think we were gonna have fun . . . but we did, didn't we?
zoegirl:	especially when u threw your ball into that truck driver's lane. (snicker, snicker)
SnowAngel:	he could have been MUCH more understanding. it's not like i meant to.
zoegirl:	and then u knocked over his beer when u went to reclaim it, ya big klutz.
zoegirl:	poor guy!
SnowAngel:	poor me! i'm under a lot of stress, zoe. i'm leaving in 6 days!!!
zoegirl:	what i don't get is why u just didn't tell him u'd spilled his beer, instead of leaving it glopped on the floor in a puddle. if u'd cleaned it up right then, nothing else would have happened.
SnowAngel:	i didn't tell him cuz i didn't want him yelling at me again. duh!
zoegirl:	well that strategy sure worked
SnowAngel:	it's not MY fault. who knew that beer would get so sticky?
zoegirl:	and who knew he'd attempt his patented foot-slide approach right after stepping smack into it?

Send   Cancel

81

SnowAngel:	i think he needs to alter his diet. a slimmer man wouldn't have fallen so hard.
zoegirl:	too many cheese fries
SnowAngel:	at least it caused a distraction as we stole our shoes. frankly, zo, i'm still surprised u went along with it.
zoegirl:	the operative word is "trade," angela. we gave them a more than fair trade.
SnowAngel:	in your case, maybe. i gave them a pair of chrissy's old tap shoes from when she used to take lessons.
zoegirl:	um, angela? why did u just insert a pirate smiley?
SnowAngel:	i dunno. cuz it's cute?
zoegirl:	ur such a goof
zoegirl:	so what r u doing for the rest of the day?
SnowAngel:	i'm PACKING. how's that for a mood killer?
zoegirl:	oh, angela
SnowAngel:	come keep me company, please-please-pleasy-please?
zoegirl:	sure, only i have to go to work at 5:00. and at some point, i should probably study for finals.
SnowAngel:	finals. *vomit* i am so unprepared. i told my mom that she was going to ruin my GPA, but did she care?
SnowAngel:	there is no way i can be expected to study when my whole life is being ripped apart.
zoegirl:	maybe we can study together after i help u pack.
SnowAngel:	just come over. i don't care what we do, as long as i'm not alone!

Sunday, December 12, 3:30 PM E.S.T.

mad maddie:	**hey, a-boogie**

SnowAngel:	hey, m-boogie
SnowAngel:	how long r u gonna stay on this "boogie" kick?
mad maddie:	**for-boogie-ever. got a problem wid dat?**
SnowAngel:	ur a freak
SnowAngel:	so wazzup?
mad maddie:	**nothing, just procrastinating. i SHOULD be studying, but let's just say i'm not.**
mad maddie:	**wanna go get krispy kremes?**
SnowAngel:	heck yeah!
mad maddie:	**boogie-licious!**

Monday, December 13, 5:23 PM E.S.T.

zoegirl:	hey, angela. guess what happened in bio today?
SnowAngel:	what?
zoegirl:	the overhead projector screen fell on mr. mack's head. he was tugging on the screen, and the whole metal tube thing swung down and clonked him on his skull.
SnowAngel:	poor mr. mack!
zoegirl:	don't worry, he's ok. but for the rest of the period he pretended to have amnesia, and every time someone asked a question about our exam, he'd be like, "what's your name again?"
SnowAngel:	that's gonna be me at my stupid new school. i won't know a single person's name except stupid glendy.
SnowAngel:	i wish I'D get clonked on my head—at least then i'd be put out of my misery.

83

ttfn

zoegirl:	angela!
zoegirl:	i told u about mr. mack to cheer u up, not make u more depressed!
SnowAngel:	oh
SnowAngel:	well . . . ha
zoegirl:	that wasn't very convincing
SnowAngel:	HAHAHAHAHA
SnowAngel:	was that better?
zoegirl:	er, thanks for trying
SnowAngel:	yeah, u 2
SnowAngel:	bye

Tuesday, December 14, 4:09 PM E.S.T.

zoegirl:	i can't believe finals start tomorrow—help!
SnowAngel:	which means only 3 more days until . . . never mind.
zoegirl:	i know
zoegirl:	that's all i can think about, even tho i've *got* to focus on studying.
SnowAngel:	there's no way i'm getting any studying done. i've just accepted it.
SnowAngel:	sorry i'm writing so slow, btw. i cut my finger on the packing tape dispenser, and the band-aid's making it hard to type.
zoegirl:	that's ok
SnowAngel:	ms. higgins gave us the question for our take-home essay. wanna hear it?

Send   Cancel

zoegirl:	sure
SnowAngel:	it's awful. it's like she WANTS to torture me, as if that was her evil plan. "using any 3 texts from this semester, discuss the following quote: 'home is where the heart is.' support your position with examples."
zoegirl:	oh man
SnowAngel:	i know
SnowAngel:	hey zo . . . do u ever just feel sad for no reason?
zoegirl:	i do, yeah.
SnowAngel:	me 2
SnowAngel:	*sigh*
SnowAngel:	guess my bracelet didn't work, huh?
zoegirl:	what bracelet?
zoegirl:	oh, your "believe" bracelet
SnowAngel:	i kept thinking that maybe this was all a joke, maybe it would all go away. i've been closing my eyes and rubbing the "believe" part, as if my wish might actually come true. isn't that stupid?
zoegirl:	not stupid at all. i wish it *had* come true.
SnowAngel:	oh well
zoegirl:	i don't want u to move, angela.
SnowAngel:	me neither ☹

Wednesday, December 15, 6:59 PM E.S.T.

zoegirl:	3 finals down, 2 to go!
SnowAngel:	😵

zoegirl:	i hear u. it's like, yay that we're over half done, but the pressure's still on.
zoegirl:	i've been mowing my way thru my mongo bag of snack-size snickers, which i've somehow convinced my mom i have to have in order to study. i don't know how it started, but now every year at exam time she stocks up on snickers and dr pepper.
SnowAngel:	while my mom, on the other hand, asks questions like, "have u cleaned out your closet yet? the moving truck will be here tomorrow afternoon, u know."
zoegirl:	do u have to be there for that? cuz maddie and i wanna take u out since it's your . . . u know.
SnowAngel:	last nite?
zoegirl:	yeah. we want to spend every minute we can with u.
SnowAngel:	at least someone does.
SnowAngel:	other than u 2, do u know that hardly ANYONE has acted the slightest bit devastated that i'm moving? they act sad for like a second, and then they're all, "omg, have u finished your take-home yet? have u memorized the formulas for chemistry?"
zoegirl:	ppl just don't know how to handle it, angela. everyone hates it that ur leaving.
SnowAngel:	it's like when u get a haircut and u go to school all self-conscious and waiting for ppl to comment on it, and then no one notices at all. that's what it's gonna be like when i'm gone.
zoegirl:	not for us, angela
zoegirl:	u will leave a hole the size of france

Send   Cancel

Wednesday, December 15, 7:12 PM E.S.T.

SnowAngel:	me again. my mom says it's fine if i go out with u guys tomorrow nite. she said she already assumed that's what i'd be doing.
zoegirl:	well that's good
SnowAngel:	i can stay out as late as i want, which i guess is nice of her.
SnowAngel:	but it's not enuff.
zoegirl:	no, it's not.
SnowAngel:	☹

Thursday, December 16, 2:02 PM E.S.T.

mad maddie: we're done!

zoegirl: yay!!!

mad maddie: do u have the candles & food & quilt?

zoegirl: i do. u have the cds and pics?

mad maddie: in my pack.

zoegirl: she's gonna cry, u know. we all r.

mad maddie: NO WE'RE NOT. c ya at collier park!

Thursday, December 16, 2:04 PM E.S.T.

mad maddie: whoot! whoot!

SnowAngel: oh god, i JUST turned my paper in. i'm the last person left in the room.

mad maddie: meet me at back parking lot!

Send   Cancel

 SnowAngel: YEAH!!!

Friday, December 17, 10:01 AM E.S.T.

zoegirl:	omg
mad maddie:	**i know**
zoegirl:	she's *gone* maddie
mad maddie:	**do u have to say it like that?**
zoegirl:	but it's the truth. as of exactly one hour ago, angela doesn't live here anymore.
mad maddie:	**i don't know how to**
mad maddie:	**i feel so**
zoegirl:	wrong?
mad maddie:	**yeah**
mad maddie:	**w/o her, everything feels wrong**

Saturday, December 18, 10:21 PM P.S.T.

SnowAngel:	well, here i am in crudballs california. i couldn't IM before now cuz stupid dad hadn't set up his computer, and my own computer won't be here until monday when the movers arrive. but i breathed down his back ALL DAY until he did it.
Auto response from zoegirl: sleeping and sad. i miss my angela!	
SnowAngel	nooo! why r u sleeping? it's not even 10:30!
SnowAngel:	oh yeah, the time difference. i'm not even in the same TIME ZONE as u anymore!
SnowAngel:	i hate this so much, zoe. i really really do.

 Send Cancel

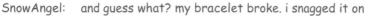

SnowAngel:	and guess what? my bracelet broke. i snagged it on the corner of the ticket counter and the leather snapped and the silver part flew off and i couldn't find it anywhere and now it's ruined, just like my whole entire life.
SnowAngel:	so just in case u were wondering, let me enlighten u:
SnowAngel:	i
SnowAngel:	don't
SnowAngel:	b
SnowAngel:	lieve

Saturday, December 18, 10:33 PM P.S.T.

SnowAngel:	maddie?
Auto response from mad maddie: zzzzz . . .	
SnowAngel:	great, even UR asleep.
SnowAngel:	maddie, i lost my "believe" bracelet. ask zoe, she'll tell u what happened.
SnowAngel:	i want it back, mads.
SnowAngel:	i want my life back.
SnowAngel:	god, i feel so alone.

Sunday, December 19, 2:11 PM E.S.T.

zoegirl:	hey, mads. i talked to angela this morning—she's incredibly sad.
mad maddie:	**when was this?**
zoegirl:	i called her as soon as i checked my messages. she'd left

Send   Cancel

89

	a zillion. we talked for an hour before my mom made me get off.
mad maddie:	**what did she have to say?**
zoegirl:	that she hates her apartment, for 1 thing. and she hates el cerrito.
zoegirl:	it's so weird imagining her in a brand-new place, isn't it? i try to tell myself it's true, but it doesn't *feel* true.
mad maddie:	**i know what u mean. i drove by her house yesterday, even tho i know i shouldn't have. it looked so . . . empty.**
zoegirl:	i bet
zoegirl:	she said she loved our moonlight picnic, tho. and the photo album. she said it's the only thing keeping her sane.
mad maddie:	**yeah, that was a good time**
zoegirl:	i don't know if i'd say it was a "good" time, but i know what u mean.
zoegirl:	i told u we'd be sobbing, tho. even u, miss i'm-so-tough-maddie. sometimes i think ur the biggest softie of us all.
mad maddie:	**oh please**
zoegirl:	i mean it in a good way
mad maddie:	**ok, well, enuff of this drama, cuz i'm off to meet chive. wanna come?**
zoegirl:	no thanks. i guess i feel more like being alone.
mad maddie:	**u deal with things your way, i'll deal with them mine.**
mad maddie:	**laters!**

Monday, December 20, 3:25 PM P.S.T.

SnowAngel:	hi, mads. FINALLY!
mad maddie:	**a-boogie! wassup?**

Send   Cancel

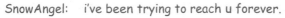

SnowAngel:	i've been trying to reach u forever.
SnowAngel:	u haven't been avoiding me, have u?
mad maddie:	**WHAT?**
SnowAngel:	u haven't IMed me, and u haven't returned my calls. i thought maybe u were sick of me cuz i'm such a downer all the time.
SnowAngel:	jk
mad maddie:	**don't be crazy—i've just been busy.**
mad maddie:	**so what's new?**
SnowAngel:	my pillow got lost in the move. isn't that just dandy? the movers arrived this morning, and my pillow wasn't in the truck!
mad maddie:	**that high-tech squishy pillow from the sleep store?**
SnowAngel:	it's the only good pillow i've ever had in my life. now i'll have to use this crap pillow that mom ran out and bought me at some crap store, and it's 1 more thing in my life that utterly sucks. it's thoroughly and wrongly fluffy, and i'm never gonna be able to sleep again, i just know it. i tried it out on my bed, and i can hear my pulse thru it!
mad maddie:	**wtf?**
SnowAngel:	it presses on my neck wrong. it jams up against my carotid artery or whatever the hell it's called, and it makes my pulse ring in my brain. thump! thump! thump! that's all i can hear!
mad maddie:	**ur losing it, chickie**
mad maddie:	**repeat after me, "it is good to have a heartbeat."**
SnowAngel:	not if u have to HEAR it all the time. i HATE hearing my pulse!

Send   Cancel   91

mad maddie:	**so sleep on your back. duh!**
SnowAngel:	i can't sleep on my back. i can only sleep on my side.
SnowAngel:	r u purposefully trying to upset me?
mad maddie:	**er, i don't wanna name names, but someone is freaking . . .**
SnowAngel:	*folds arms over chest* zoe would understand.
mad maddie:	**then why don't u tell HER?**
SnowAngel:	maddie! that's not very supportive!
mad maddie:	**1 sec, something just came on tv that i wanna watch**
SnowAngel:	ur watching tv while i pour my heart out? tv's more important than ME?
SnowAngel:	maddie?
SnowAngel:	maddie!!!
mad maddie:	**good god, i just saw THE most horrifying newsclip. u can catch on fire at the gas station if u touch the gas pump with 2 much static electricity—did u know that? they showed this girl putting the nozzle in her gas tank thingie, and then she got back in her car while it was pumping. she was wearing a sweater, and apparently it rubbed against the seat and got her all staticky. she went back to grab the pump . . . and KAPOW! she burst into flames!**
SnowAngel:	is this supposed to cheer me up? "sorry u lost your pillow, but at least u avoided self-immolation"?
mad maddie:	**sweater girl survived, but the news guy said that other people have actually died. damn.**
mad maddie:	**u be careful, u hear?**
SnowAngel:	why do i need to be careful? i don't even have a car. i

Send   Cancel

wanted a car, but instead i got to move to california. remember?

mad maddie: **well when and if u DO get a car, don't get back in it while ur in the middle of pumping gas. and touch the side of the car before u grab the gas pump again. that way the static electricity will flow out of u.**

SnowAngel: thanks for the tip *regards friend sourly*

SnowAngel: do u have anything else to say?

mad maddie: **umm . . . don't wear fluffy sweaters when u go to the gas station?**

SnowAngel: gbye, maddie. u r no help at all!

Tuesday, December 21, 10:30 AM E.S.T.

zoegirl: hey, angela. is it 2 early for me to be IMing u? i can never remember what the time change is.

Auto response from SnowAngel: "City sidewalks, busy sidewalks, dressed in holiday style! In the air there's a feeling of Christmas!" NOT!!! ☹

zoegirl: oh. er . . . sorry.

zoegirl: anyway, i just wanted to tell u that i mailed your present today, so u should get it soon, hopefully by christmas eve.

zoegirl: i love u, angela! IM me!!!

Wednesday, December 22, 4:43 PM P.S.T.

SnowAngel: hey, zo. sorry i missed u yesterday—i was sleeping in. it's like all i do is sleep these days, and i'm STILL tired.

Send   Cancel

zoegirl:	that's ok. i would have called u back last nite, but i picked up a shift at Kidding Around.
SnowAngel:	was doug there?
zoegirl:	he was, yeah
SnowAngel:	i had a dream about him, isn't that weird? it was actually about BOTH of u. u had dyed your hair blond to impress him.
SnowAngel:	which leads me to ask: u haven't started liking him, have u?
zoegirl:	*angela*
SnowAngel:	i'm sorry, i'm sorry *grimaces*
SnowAngel:	why am i so needy? is it just cuz i'm stuck 3,000 miles away from u guys, and i feel like everything's being torn apart?
zoegirl:	ur being silly. nothing's being torn apart.
SnowAngel:	i hope not
SnowAngel:	so have i mentioned that life sucks? i told my mom AGAIN that i wanna move back to atlanta and live with my aunt sadie, but she was like, "u haven't given california a chance. ur gonna love it, u'll c."
zoegirl:	maybe u will. i can c u as a california girl, all tan and beautiful. hey—maybe u'll learn to surf!
SnowAngel:	???
zoegirl:	sorry. just trying to be optimistic.
SnowAngel:	u know what i miss that i didn't even realize i was gonna miss? magnolia trees. i never knew how much i loved them until i moved to this barren wasteland.
zoegirl:	i love magnolia trees 2

Send   Cancel

SnowAngel:	plus i hate our stupid apartment. i still have boxes all over my room. isn't that depressing? it's like i can't bear to make myself unpack.
zoegirl:	tell me more about your apartment. i wanna be able to visualize u.
SnowAngel:	it's tiny. it's beige. there's crudballs wallpaper in my room with stupid rosebuds on it, and i can hear traffic thru my window. mom says rentals here r super expensive and we're lucky dad found a 3-bedroom place, but i disagree.
zoegirl:	have u met anybody else who lives there?
SnowAngel:	no, and i don't want to. the family below us has a kid, but she's 5. she speaks korean.
zoegirl:	she's 5 yrs old and she speaks korean? impressive.
SnowAngel:	yeah, only she doesn't speak english—that's my point. she speaks korean cuz she IS korean.
zoegirl:	oh
zoegirl:	well . . .
SnowAngel:	yes, zoe? if u can put a positive spin on my sucky life, then believe me, i wanna hear it.
zoegirl:	um . . . at least it's almost christmas?
SnowAngel:	at least it's almost christmas. *sigh*

Thursday, December 23, 6:02 PM E.S.T.

mad maddie:	**dude! chive gave me a nickel bag of pot to celebrate the birth of christ. isn't that righteous?**
SnowAngel:	what a guy

Send	Cancel

SnowAngel:	but don't u think that's the slightest bit sacreligious?
mad maddie:	**i gave him this cool marble pipe i bought at the head store in little five points. oh, and a cd he's been wanting. we're gonna make use of it all tomorrow nite—if i can escape the fam.**
SnowAngel:	maddie, tomorrow's christmas eve. u can't smoke pot on christmas eve!
mad maddie:	**why not? the 3 wise men followed a frickin STAR all the way to bethlehem. ur telling me they weren't under the influence of a certain illegal substance?**
SnowAngel:	tsk, tsk
SnowAngel:	i think u need to start going to church with zoe, young lady!
mad maddie:	**yeah, that'll happen**
SnowAngel:	so does this mean u've learned how to do it so that it doesn't hurt? the pot?
mad maddie:	**i wouldn't say that, exactly. that's why i bought the pipe—it's supposed to make it a smoother ride. but anything'll get better the more u do it, right?**
SnowAngel:	uh, i guess
mad maddie:	**it's bound 2**
mad maddie:	**btw, chive says u can score some really good pot in california, so keep your eye out for me.**
SnowAngel:	yeah, that's what i need, to get busted for drugs on top of everything else.
mad maddie:	**whine, whine, whine. nobody actually gets busted for buying pot. they only hassle u if ur a big-time cocaine dealer or something.**
SnowAngel:	omg, u haven't tried COCAINE, have u?

 Send Cancel

mad maddie:	angela, chill. pot is my drug of choice, thank u very much.
mad maddie:	so check it out: i picked out your christmas present 2. wanna know what it is?
SnowAngel:	a totally rockin marble pipe?
mad maddie:	haha. no, microwavable slippers.
SnowAngel:	aw, maddie, thanks!
SnowAngel:	and what, exactly, will i do with these microwavable slippers?
mad maddie:	microwave them, of course! the bottoms have these pouches of rice or beans or something in them, and when u microwave them, they get roasty-toasty. they're for cold feet, u goof.
SnowAngel:	ooo, they sound wonderful. it gets really chilly here at nite, like unbelievably so. and our apartment is always freezing.
mad maddie:	i'll put them in the mail tomorrow—that is, unless i don't. but i'll mail them soon, i promise.
SnowAngel:	no rush. i haven't even picked out anything for u or zoe.
mad maddie:	so what's up with zoe these days? i haven't seen her all vacation.
SnowAngel:	why not?
mad maddie:	dunno, just haven't. it's not for any BAD reason.
SnowAngel:	well, she's fine. she's working a lot, it sounds like.
SnowAngel:	with doug
mad maddie:	why do u say it like that, "with doug"?
SnowAngel:	i dunno. i can't get him out of my mind—isn't that weird? i even had a dream about him the other nite.

Send Cancel

SnowAngel:	u don't think there's anything going on b/w him and zoe, do u?
mad maddie:	**why, did zoe say there was?**
SnowAngel:	no, of course not. i'm just being silly.
mad maddie:	**listen, i've g2g. i've gotta stash my pot somewhere so the moms won't find it. i'm thinking the box from the set of "thank u" notes u gave me when we were 13—once i throw out the actual cards, that is.**
SnowAngel:	gee, i'm touched
mad maddie:	**why did u give those to me, anywayz? i mean, c'mon. thank u notes?**
SnowAngel:	i don't know, cuz the notes were cute. they were decorated with strawberries.
SnowAngel:	why do u still have them???
mad maddie:	**uh, cuz the notes r cute and they're decorated with strawberries? which translates into: never gonna use 'em, no sir, no how?**
mad maddie:	**but the box makes a PERFECT hiding spot for my pot.**
SnowAngel:	cute little strawberries, cute little baggie of pot . . .
mad maddie:	**it's the organic theme—yeah!**

Friday, December 24, 3:33 PM P.S.T.

SnowAngel:	zoe, your present came in the mail today! thank u so much!!!
zoegirl:	u r so welcome!
zoegirl:	do u like it?
SnowAngel:	it's beautiful. SHE'S beautiful, i should say. i put her

	on my bedside table so i can c her first thing when i wake up. she's the only decoration in my entire room.
zoegirl:	she's the angel of hope, which u probably already know if u looked at the sticker on the bottom. i know it's dorky, but . . . i dunno. i thought it would be kinda like your "believe" bracelet, altho it's not something to wear.
SnowAngel:	aww, zoe, ur so sweet
zoegirl:	i looked for another "believe" bracelet, btw. i went to the store where u got it, but i couldn't find anything like it.
SnowAngel:	cuz it was the only 1. ever.
SnowAngel:	but THANK U for my angel. i love her, love her, love her. *sends big smoochy kisses to dear friend zoe*
zoegirl:	plus, the whole "angel" thing, with u being SnowAngel and all.
SnowAngel:	she's great, zoe. god knows i need all the angels i can get.
zoegirl:	i almost got 1 for me, 2, but then i thought, "no, it should just be something special for angela."
SnowAngel:	we can share her, how bout that?
zoegirl:	yay!
SnowAngel:	so whenever u think of doing something bad, u can remember that she's watching over u from california, and u can change your erring ways. ☺
zoegirl:	haha
zoegirl:	can u believe it's christmas eve?
SnowAngel:	no, i thoroughly cannot. i haven't done ANY shopping, which for my family is just 2 damn bad. but for u and maddie, i feel terrible.

Send   Cancel

99

zoegirl:	please don't, u've got enuff to worry about. seriously, we don't care in the slightest.
SnowAngel:	but i do
SnowAngel:	hey, i know! i'll mail ME back to atlanta for your present!
zoegirl:	yeah!!!
SnowAngel:	how much does a plane ticket cost, u think? i've got $250 in savings. is that enuff?
zoegirl:	i don't know, i bet it's a little more than that.
zoegirl:	r u really thinking about coming?
SnowAngel:	i doubt my parents would let me. ☺
SnowAngel:	but if it's my money, then i can do what i want, right?
zoegirl:	er . . .
SnowAngel:	i'm gonna go check plane fares.
SnowAngel:	don't worry, i'm not REALLY gonna take off w/o my parents' permission, but it would be good info to have in the back of my brain—just in case.
zoegirl:	just in case what?
SnowAngel:	what's that one website called? travel-something-or-other?
SnowAngel:	oh well, i'll figure it out. bye!

Saturday, December 25, 1:01 PM P.S.T.

SnowAngel:	merry christmas, zoe!!!
zoegirl:	merry christmas!!!
SnowAngel:	guess what? my mom and dad upgraded my phone plan so that i have 1,000 anytime minutes a month!!! i told

Send   Cancel

them it was the best christmas present ever—other than moving back to atlanta, that is. so now i can actually call u guys and not worry about it so much! *cha cha cha*

zoegirl:	so why r u IMing? call me, u goof!
SnowAngel:	it doesn't kick in til january. what about u? get anything good?
zoegirl:	stocks and bonds as usual from my very exciting parents. and some earrings. but, whatever. i just love christmas in general.
SnowAngel:	me 2. this is the happiest i've been since we moved. my mom made cinnamon rolls for breakfast, and our tree looks so beautiful, even tho it's not nearly as big as the one we had last year. and tomorrow we're gonna drive into the city for the after-christmas sales.
zoegirl:	cool
zoegirl:	when u say "the city," do u mean san francisco?
SnowAngel:	yeah, ppl here just call it the city. anyway, we're gonna get a hotel room and stay for a couple of nites, do some of the tourist-y stuff. so i might be out of touch for a while.
zoegirl:	actually, i will 2. we're going to my grandmom's house. we won't be back til wednesday.
SnowAngel:	and maddie's already left for her aunt's house. she was planning on taking her stash with her, did she tell u?
zoegirl:	her "stash"?
zoegirl:	of what?

SnowAngel:	of pot. that's what chive gave her for christmas. *eyes roll*
zoegirl:	is she actually gonna *smoke* it?
zoegirl:	oh man, angela. i think it's really bad that she's getting high in normal situations.
SnowAngel:	she said it's a coping mechanism based on years of family tradition, just that her relatives use alcohol instead of pot. and then she was like, "not that i have anything against alcohol, don't get me wrong . . . "
zoegirl:	u should tell her how dumb she's being
SnowAngel:	what do u mean, i should? ur the 1 who's still in town with her!
zoegirl:	yeah, but *ur* the 1 she talks to about this stuff. she never brings it up with me.
SnowAngel:	cuz she knows u'd yell at her, probably
SnowAngel:	anyway, it's christmas. i didn't wanna spoil the mood.
zoegirl:	i bet she's doing it to impress chive some more. so that when she gets back in town, she can be like, "hey, i smoked the stash u gave me."
SnowAngel:	no, here's what she'd say: "duuuuude, righteous weed."
zoegirl:	i don't like it. it worries me.
SnowAngel:	it worries me 2
SnowAngel:	so . . .
zoegirl:	so . . . ?
SnowAngel:	so we'll tell her, ok? for real, w/o holding back
zoegirl:	yeah, ok
zoegirl:	bye!

Send   Cancel

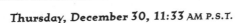

Thursday, December 30, 11:33 AM P.S.T.

SnowAngel:	madigan, long time no talk! how was your aunt's?
mad maddie:	**hey, a. 1 sec while i finish this email . . .**
mad maddie:	**ok, i'm back. i was responding to a delta airlines customer service dude, btw. still no word on your bracelet.**
SnowAngel:	u emailed delta about my bracelet? aw, mads, i didn't know u cared!
mad maddie:	**he checked their claim area, but no "believe" thingie.**
SnowAngel:	damn
SnowAngel:	but that was incredibly sweet of u to try
mad maddie:	**yeah, i know**
SnowAngel:	so did u have a good time with your relatives?
mad maddie:	**the usual. the cousins breathed garlic in my face, the dads got ripped and made fart jokes.**
mad maddie:	**but who cares about that. i wanna hear about U! how was the city?!!**
SnowAngel:	oh, maddie, it was AWESOME. the only un-awesome thing was that u and zoe weren't there, cuz u guys would have loved it. there's so much going on—omg, it's so different from atlanta. OR el cerrito, which doesn't even compare.
SnowAngel:	there was this street musician on the sidewalk who totally made me think of u. he played the guitar, and he had a harmonica on a frame by his mouth, and he had cymbals strapped to his knees. i was like, "maddie would love this guy."

ttfn

mad maddie:	**sounds cool. atlanta is pretty boring when it comes to street life.**
SnowAngel:	san francisco is definitely not boring. there r ppl EVERYWHERE. vendors selling jewelry, hot dog stands, guys with knock-off watches. oh, and we went to chinatown, which was sooooo fun. u go thru this archway thing, and it's like stepping into a different world. everyone was chinese—der—and they had these cute little shops with satin slippers and sparkly barrettes. tourist-y stuff 2, like miniature trolley cars and I HEART SAN FRANCISCO shirts.
mad maddie:	**did ya get me 1? did ya, did ya?**
SnowAngel:	sorry, no tacky souvenir shirt
mad maddie:	**damn. chive loves that campy stuff.**
SnowAngel:	i got u something better. i got u lots of stuff, actually—u and zoe both. from chinatown i got u guys candy, like Hello Kitty suckers and gum in weird flavors like cantaloupe and blueberry. and from the ferry building, which is this place down on the waterfront, i got u both boxes of the most awesome chocolates in the world, called scharffen berger chocolates. i got u a mix-and-match assortment with infusions of lavender and chile—which sounds gross, but it's not—and i got zoe a box of these super thin pear slices dipped in dark chocolate. i hope u guys like them.
mad maddie:	**we will, i'm sure. thanks, a.**
SnowAngel:	and btw, i LOVE my slippers. i've got them on right now.
mad maddie:	**did u microwave them?**

Send   Cancel

104

SnowAngel:	i did. chrissy was like, "ew, what's that smell? it smells like burnt straw!"
mad maddie:	**hey now—the guy said they were supposed to smell good!**
SnowAngel:	i like the smell, it's just chrissy who doesn't. anyway it doesn't matter, cuz they feel so lovely and warm. 🙂
mad maddie:	**i'm glad u like them. and i'm glad ur doing better in the land of california.**
mad maddie:	**u R doing better, right?**
SnowAngel:	i dunno. a LITTLE, i guess.
mad maddie:	**take it and run with it, girl. u deserve it.**
SnowAngel:	except school starts on tuesday. that's 5 days away!
mad maddie:	**nyah, nyah! u have to start a day earlier than we do!**
SnowAngel:	i just hope all the girls aren't like glendy. i have to spend tomorrow nite with her, cuz mr. boss invited our whole family over for new year's eve, and of course my dad said yes.
SnowAngel:	can u imagine a worse way to ring in the new year? i begged my dad to let me stay home, but he refused.
mad maddie:	**bastard**
SnowAngel:	what about u? what r u gonna do for new year's?
mad maddie:	**i'm hanging with my man chive, and probably meade and brannen and whitney. we're going to a concert at the omni. it's a battle of the bands.**
SnowAngel:	huh. r whitney and chive still an item?
mad maddie:	**do u know how much he would hate it if he heard u call them that? an "item"?**
SnowAngel:	so r they?

Send   Cancel   105

mad maddie:	i guess, altho they can't be THAT serious, cuz sometimes chive and i still fool around. like yesterday we were on a beer run, and at a stoplight he just leaned over and kissed me out of the blue. a LONG kiss.
SnowAngel:	and u let him?
mad maddie:	what do u mean "let" him?
mad maddie:	whitney may be his girlfriend, but that's just cuz . . . i dunno. cuz she's pretty. cuz she does the girl thing and pouts when he doesn't call her. but i'm the 1 he talks to about music and life and shit. we've got, like, a connection.
SnowAngel:	hmmm
SnowAngel:	but then—don't be mad—why does he make u hide it?
mad maddie:	give me a break. we're not into rules, angela. the world is bigger than that.
SnowAngel:	oh
mad maddie:	what does that mean?
SnowAngel:	nothing!
mad maddie:	yes it does. u said it like u don't believe it, i can tell.
SnowAngel:	did u smoke the bag of pot he gave u?
mad maddie:	as a matter of fact i did. do u have a problem with that, 2?
mad maddie:	it's just POT, angela. nobody's gonna get hurt from a little pot.
SnowAngel:	if u say so
SnowAngel:	just. . . be careful, all right?
mad maddie:	i'm having fun, angela. be happy for me.
SnowAngel:	ok, ok
mad maddie:	good luck tomorrow nite with glendy. call and tell me how it goes!

106

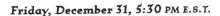

Friday, December 31, 5:30 PM E.S.T.

zoegirl: helloooo! i can't chat for long—i've got to get ready for tonite—but i wanted to talk to u one last time before the new year. is that dorky or what? i'm turning into my grandmom, who always calls on the nite before my bday and says, "i just wanted to talk to u one last time while ur 15, honey."

SnowAngel: awww

SnowAngel: what r u getting ready for? do u have big new year's eve plans?

zoegirl: oh

zoegirl: um, not really, just a party

SnowAngel: a party? with who?

zoegirl: actually, it's not a party, it's more like ppl r just gonna hang out from work.

zoegirl: it's no big deal

SnowAngel: will doug be there?

zoegirl: huh, i dunno

zoegirl: but i wish i was doing something with *u* instead. u and maddie, that is. like last year when we made chocolate fondue and maddie fondued a tomato. remember?

SnowAngel: u could still do something with her even tho i'm not there.

SnowAngel: why aren't u?

zoegirl: cuz we both have plans already, i guess

SnowAngel: i think that's lame. have u seen her at all this whole vacation?

Send   Cancel

ttfn

zoegirl:	well, we've both been out of town
SnowAngel:	i talked to her about chive, btw
zoegirl:	u did? what did she say?
SnowAngel:	she got defensive, which i guess was to be expected. and then i felt bad for bringing it up. and then . . . i dunno. i decided to let it go.
zoegirl:	angela!
SnowAngel:	i don't wanna spend my time with her arguing—i get so little time with her as it is.
SnowAngel:	anyway, it's her life, right? she knows what she's doing.
zoegirl:	does she?
SnowAngel:	as much as any of us, i guess
SnowAngel:	bye!

Saturday, January 1, 11:34 AM E.S.T.

zoegirl:	mads! happy new year!
mad maddie:	**oof, if u say so**
mad maddie:	**can we talk later? i'm kinda hurting here.**
zoegirl:	hurting how? r u hungover?
mad maddie:	**maybe just a tad**
zoegirl:	just chat with me for a sec. it's important.
mad maddie:	**well in that case, of course. wassup?**
zoegirl:	i have something to tell u, that's all. it's about . . .
mad maddie:	**yessss?**
zoegirl:	hold on, 1st let me ask u something. things aren't weird b/w us, r they?

Send   Cancel

mad maddie:	**huh?**
zoegirl:	angela thinks it's strange that we haven't seen each other much over vacation. but that's just cuz we've been busy, right?
mad maddie:	**duh. why else?**
zoegirl:	right, right. i just wanted to make sure.
mad maddie:	**so what's going on that u need to talk about?**
zoegirl:	aaargh. it's about doug. we kinda . . . hung out together last nite.
mad maddie:	**oh yeah? did u go to a new year's eve party?**
zoegirl:	no, it was just the 2 of us.
mad maddie:	**as in a DATE?**
mad maddie:	**uh oh. does angela know?**
zoegirl:	er . . . that's part of the problem.
mad maddie:	**yeah, i'll say. angela's gonna think u purposely waited til she was gone, and then BAM! u stole her man.**
zoegirl:	he's not "her man." god!
mad maddie:	**well, is he YOUR man?**
zoegirl:	that's the other part of the problem. cuz i don't know, maddie. i just don't know!
mad maddie:	**explain**
zoegirl:	well, we went to dinner at La Fonda, and that was great. i love their guacamole. and then neither of us wanted to go home, so we went and hung out in the basement of trinity church. doug's an acolyte, so he's got the key to the youth group lounge.
mad maddie:	**oh god, zoe. again?**
zoegirl:	what do u mean, again?

mad maddie:	this doesn't ring any bells for u? any CHURCH bells, per chance?
zoegirl:	what r u talking about?
mad maddie:	oh, nothing. definitely not a certain holy-roller teacher of yore . . .
zoegirl:	do u wanna hear my story or not?
mad maddie:	by all means, pray continue
zoegirl:	we were sitting there talking, and it was chilly, so doug told me to come sit on the couch with him cuz it would be warmer. so i did, and . . . we kissed.
mad maddie:	holy cow
zoegirl:	that's not all. we *kept* kissing . . . and kissing and kissing and kissing. and it's not like i was swept away or anything, but at the same time i didn't stop him, u know? i didn't wanna hurt his feelings.
mad maddie:	u didn't wanna hurt his feelings? u did NOT just say that, zoe.
zoegirl:	anyway, we somehow ended up with both our shirts practically off, but not completely. they were just pushed up really high.
zoegirl:	actually, i was wearing my vandy sweatshirt—and i wasn't wearing a bra underneath.
mad maddie:	whoa, zoe! u hussy!
zoegirl:	i know! i'm sure he was pretty startled. but i didn't *plan* it that way—it just happened!
mad maddie:	and in the church basement, no less. what is it with u and jesus? does he, like, turn u on?
zoegirl:	can we let go of that, please? i knew u would have to say that, and now u have, so that's over.

110

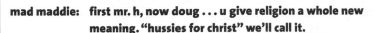

mad maddie:	**first mr. h, now doug . . . u give religion a whole new meaning. "hussies for christ" we'll call it.**
zoegirl:	what if doug *does* think i'm a hussy? what if he woke up this morning and was like, "there's something wrong with her?"
zoegirl:	we did more last nite than i've ever done with *anyone*. what if he looks down on me now?
mad maddie:	**zoe, u r so insane i can hardly stand it. i'm sure he went home with a stiffie, while visions of zoe danced in his head.**
zoegirl:	i just wish i didn't feel guilty. why do i feel guilty?!
mad maddie:	**i have nooooo idea. all u did is fool around.**
mad maddie:	**ooo, do u think u made his scrotum tighten?**
zoegirl:	*what*?
mad maddie:	**chive's been reading james joyce, and apparently there's something in one of his books about some guy's scrotum tightening. it cracked me up.**
zoegirl:	ok, i'm not even going there. please do not talk about . . . that particular part of the body in reference to doug ever again, all right?
mad maddie:	**doug has a scrotum, doug has a scrotum!**
zoegirl:	i mean it, maddie
mad maddie:	**cuz u think it's DIRTY? cuz u think it's NASTY?**
mad maddie:	**god, zoe, u need to learn how to relax if ur gonna have a boyfriend.**
zoegirl:	i don't think any of those things. i just think that not everything is a joke, and that fooling around should count for something. it shouldn't be a free-for-all.

Send   Cancel   111

zoegirl:	maybe that's something *u* need to learn if *ur* ever gonna have a boyfriend.
zoegirl:	maddie? u still there?
mad maddie:	**nothing like a cold dose of reality from one of your best friends, eh, zo?**
zoegirl:	maddie . . .
mad maddie:	**no need to hold back, u know. just tell me how u really feel.**
zoegirl:	look, u started it
zoegirl:	but i didn't tell u about doug so that u and i could get into a fight. i told u cuz of *angela*. what am i supposed to do about angela?
mad maddie:	**2 words, zoe, and i've said 'em before: TELL HER, U IDIOT.**
zoegirl:	that's 4 words
mad maddie:	**i am giving u the bird right now, just so u know**
zoegirl:	ack—she just popped up on my buddy list!! i'm not ready to talk to her yet, so i'm gonna log off. bye!

Saturday, January 1, 9:01 AM P.S.T.

SnowAngel:	hola, maddie. happy new year!
mad maddie:	**same to u, a-boogie**
SnowAngel:	were u just talking to zoe? her name was on my buddy list for a millisecond, but now it's gone.
mad maddie:	**huh, fancy that**
SnowAngel:	so how was your new year's eve??? any smoochy-smoochy action with chive???
mad maddie:	**ixnay on the oochie-smoochy-say . . . at least b/w me and**

	chive. altho SOMEONE was smoochy-smoochy-ing last nite, i can tell u that.
SnowAngel:	oh yeah? who?
mad maddie:	**er . . . no one in particular. i just mean that surely someone was getting it on, cuz after all it was new year's eve, right?**
SnowAngel:	r u just being random? cuz sometimes i don't know what ur talking about.
mad maddie:	**forget it. yeah, i was being random.**
SnowAngel:	so how was the concert?
mad maddie:	**the bands sucked, but we had a blast. this 1 band played a cover of "stairway to heaven," and we flipped open our cell phones and waved them over our heads like lighters. we started a whole trend.**
SnowAngel:	ha—that's awesome
mad maddie:	**isn't it? by the end of the song u could c glowing lights from 1 end of the amphitheater to the other.**
mad maddie:	**anywayz, chive bought us all beers with his fake, so we were verrrrry happy. at least until chive spilled his on the guy in front of us, who happened to be bald. the guy whipped around all mad and fuming, and i was like, "oh, shit! sorry, man!"**
SnowAngel:	what did chive do?
mad maddie:	**he just sat there cracking up. i was elbowing him and going, "dude, U spilled it!" but he fully let me take the blame. it was hilarious.**
SnowAngel:	oh, yeah. it sounds hilarious. *deadpans to show hilarity*
mad maddie:	**but i'm hurting today, i'll tell u.**

Send   Cancel

SnowAngel:	well that's 2 bad
SnowAngel:	but i don't feel sorry for u, wanna know why? cuz while u were out whupping it up with chive, i was trapped in glendy's room watching "The Sisterhood of the Traveling Pants" on pay-per-view.
mad maddie:	**i thought u liked that movie**
SnowAngel:	correction, i LOVE that movie—almost as much as i love "A Cinderella Story."
SnowAngel:	but it's only meant to be seen with u and zoe. i mean, c'mon. 4 girls, friends forever? that's US, mads, except there's only 3 of us.
mad maddie:	**and we're cooler. and we say words like "fuck."**
SnowAngel:	u, maybe. zoe and i r more refined. *adopts snooty expression and sips from teacup*
mad maddie:	**fuck, fuck, fuck**
SnowAngel:	but it wasn't just the choice of movie, altho that WAS the most horrible awful irony imaginable. it was the fact that glendy was such a baby about it. 1st she asked her mom if we could order it, and her mom said no, so then she worked up these fake tears and was all, "oh, daddy, please? i never get to do anything. please, daddy, please?"
mad maddie:	**and her dad gave in? bad move, buster.**
SnowAngel:	i know. she is such an only child.
mad maddie:	**ha. like zoe?**
SnowAngel:	no, cuz zoe's parents r strict.
SnowAngel:	i guess it's possible that glendy's mom is 2, but it makes no difference since mr. boss gives in whenever she pretends to cry.

mad maddie: r u sure she's 16 and not 6?

SnowAngel: omg, exactly!

SnowAngel: she kept talking through the whole movie—of course she's a movie-talker—and she was like, "i'm lena, the beautiful 1. she's so me."

SnowAngel: and i was like, "uh, no, ur bailey, the annoying kid who leeched onto tibby. only bailey turned out to be cool, and u r the epitome of un-cool."

mad maddie: maybe glendy'll get a terminal disease like balley did

SnowAngel: maddie!

mad maddie: those sisterhood chicks wouldn't say that either, i know. but it made u laff, didn't it?

SnowAngel: anyway, i couldn't get away from glendy fast enuff. and yet, this is who i get to go to school with on tuesday, cuz maddie, we're CARPOOLING!!! mr. boss is gonna drop us off each morning so my mom can drive chrissy to junior high.

mad maddie: christ, angela

mad maddie: u better just move back here. hop on that plane like u said.

SnowAngel: plane fares cost more than i thought, tho. the cheapest was $454, which is $200 too much. *grrr*

mad maddie: that sucks

SnowAngel: maybe i should ask glendy for a loan, or rather, get her to ask her daddy for 1. what do u think?

mad maddie: i think u need to give the glendinizer the boot. just quit talking to her, she'll get the message.

SnowAngel: like i can do that when we're squished together in the same car every freaking morning.

Send   Cancel

mad maddie:	oh—i have to tell u 1 more funny thing that happened at the concert. whitney and i had to pee, but the line in the ladies' room was ridiculously long as usual. so whitney starts whining about how she REALLY has to go, and i'm like, "what do u want me to do about it?" she goes, "i dunno. something!" so i clapped my hands super loud and said, "listen up, ladies. 10 seconds apiece! that's your limit!"
SnowAngel:	oh god, maddie
SnowAngel:	and how did u enforce this limit?
mad maddie:	i started counting down from 10 to 1 each time someone stepped into a stall. at first ppl just stared at me, but then this big ol' trucker gal with a beer belly started chanting with me, and then other ppl in the line joined in 2.
SnowAngel:	did it work?
mad maddie:	u bet it did. that was the best part. girls started charging out of the stalls with their pants unzipped, trying to beat the clock. this 1 woman yelled, "i need 20! i had dinner at Max's Burritos!"
SnowAngel:	good lord
mad maddie:	heh heh heh
SnowAngel:	i hope whitney appreciated your gesture of goodwill.
mad maddie:	r u kidding? she was mortified. AND she took longer than her allotted 10 seconds. she got booed by trucker gal.
SnowAngel:	ha!
SnowAngel:	i can so c that whole scene. it makes me miss u, mads.
mad maddie:	i miss u 2, a
SnowAngel:	it's not fair that i have to spend new year's day alone

Send   Cancel

mad maddie:	**well, do something nice for yourself.**
SnowAngel:	like what?
mad maddie:	**i dunno, whatever u feel like doing. and now i've g2g, cuz it's time for a little nappie. byeas!**

Saturday, January 1, 4:42 PM P.S.T.

SnowAngel:	zoe, where r u??? i can't get hold of u no matter how hard i try! why is your cell turned off, u goof?
Autoresponse from zoegirl:	happy new year, everyone! the world is full of possibilities!
SnowAngel:	not for me, it's not. *pouts*
SnowAngel:	HOWEVER. i am gonna take maddie's advice and do something fun for a change. i've snagged a bottle of the champagne mom and dad bought for last nite—don't worry, it's mini-size, just right for me!—and i'm about to pop "A Cinderella Story" into the DVD player.
SnowAngel:	i just wish u and mads were here to watch it with me!

Saturday, January 1, 6:01 PM P.S.T.

SnowAngel:	zooo-eeee! oh, zoooo-eeee! where r u, girl?
Autoresponse from zoegirl:	happy new year, everyone! the world is full of possibilities!
SnowAngel:	is it? then can i be hilary duff, please, and get to kiss chad michael murray?
SnowAngel:	i think i'm a little tipsy. tee hee.
SnowAngel:	I NEED SOMEONE TO KISS!!!

Send   Cancel

SnowAngel:	do u think doug would kiss me, if he were here? i think he would. i even thought about kissing him before i left. did u know that?
SnowAngel:	hmm, i think i'll give him a ring-a-ling. *wink, wink*
SnowAngel:	ta!

Sunday, January 2, 10:54 AM E.S.T.

zoegirl:	oh shit. oh shit shit shit shit shit!
zoegirl:	have u, by any chance, talked to angela?
mad maddie:	**not since yesterday. why?**
zoegirl:	did u tell her about me and doug? and don't lie!
mad maddie:	**chill! i didn't tell her, i swear.**
zoegirl:	then how did she know? why did she pick last nite, of all the nites in the world, to suddenly ring doug up and offer herself to him? huh???
mad maddie:	**holy crap, what r u talking about?**
zoegirl:	she drank some champagne and got all mushy watching "A Cinderella Story," from what i can tell. and then for some reason she called up doug, out of the blue, and said things like, "hey, doug. do u miss me? cuz i miss u!" and "if u were here, i would kiss u. i should have a long time ago!"
mad maddie:	**this is NOT good**
zoegirl:	and now doug's all weirded out cuz it was obvious to him that angela didn't know about us, cuz if she did then why would she be hitting on him, and he doesn't understand why i haven't told her.

zoegirl:	and angela . . . well, who knows how angela's doing.
zoegirl:	shit, shit, shit!
mad maddie:	**i warned u that this was gonna happen. u know i did.**
zoegirl:	could u possibly say something the least bit supportive? i didn't plan this. it just happened!
mad maddie:	**sure, that's what U say, cuz ur the 1 who screwed up. can i just tell u how happy i am that it's u for once and not me?**
zoegirl:	u know what? ur not helping. it's like . . . god, it's like ur enjoying this!
mad maddie:	**i'm not "enjoying" it, zoe. get real.**
zoegirl:	i've gtg
mad maddie:	**wait! what did doug say to angela after she threw herself at him? u never told me!**
zoegirl:	tough. guess i'm 2 much of a screw-up, huh?
mad maddie:	**zoe!!!!!!**

Sunday, January 2, 11:13 AM E.S.T.

zoegirl:	hi, angela. it's me, your friend, who is so so sorry about . . . u know.
Auto Response from SnowAngel:	the world is NOT full of possibilities if every single possibility sucks! and u know what? i'm glad i moved to california, cuz at least california isn't full of big fat liars!!!!
zoegirl:	i am the big fat liar ur talking about? i guess i am, huh?
zoegirl:	but angela . . .
zoegirl:	aaargh

zoegirl:	i should have told u about me and doug. i know that. but i just . . . i don't know.
zoegirl:	anyway, nothing *had* happened b/w doug and me when u and i talked about it, so i wasn't actually lying. and the only reason i didn't mention it later is cuz i didn't wanna hurt u.
zoegirl:	and c'mon, if u hadn't been so jealous in the 1st place . . .
zoegirl:	never mind
zoegirl:	i'm sorry, angela. i really am!!!

Sunday, January 2, 8:20 AM P.S.T.

SnowAngel:	hi, maddie. i just got the lamest IM from zoe, which of course i didn't bother to reply to. did she tell u what happened? with doug?
mad maddie:	**yes, she told me that u've been a very naughty girl. did u drink and dial, young lady????**
SnowAngel:	WHAT?
SnowAngel:	this is NOT about me. it's about ZOE! i'm never gonna forgive her as long as i live.
mad maddie:	**well, we both know that's not true. but we can pretend if you like.**
SnowAngel:	i'm serious, maddie. she's all, "i didn't wanna hurt u, blah, blah, blah," but come on. am i so needy and pathetic that i can't even handle the truth?
mad maddie:	**hmm. do u really want me to answer that?**
SnowAngel:	she even had the nerve to blame it on me! cuz i was

Send   Cancel

	"jealous," that's why she didn't tell me about her and doug. is that not the most ridiculous thing u've ever heard?
mad maddie:	**yes, it's the most ridiculous thing i've ever heard, and yes, she should have told u. i told her that a thousand times. and now she's completely freaked that ur mad, but i told her, "sorry, zo, u brought it on yourself."**
SnowAngel:	thank u. i needed to hear that. i mean, it would have been different if
SnowAngel:	wait a minute—U knew 2?
mad maddie:	**about zoe and doug? uh . . .**
SnowAngel:	u knew they were a couple and u didn't tell me?!!!
SnowAngel:	omg, how long has this been going on???
mad maddie:	**now listen. IT WASN'T MY PLACE TO TELL. i told zoe she was screwing up, but that was her decision. i'm not her mommy, angela. i'm not either of your mommies.**
SnowAngel:	nice, maddie. try and shift the responsibility. do u not have any conscience at all?
SnowAngel:	obviously not, or u would have told your best friend that your other best friend was dating a certain person who someone else still happened to like!
mad maddie:	**that's crap, angela. u didn't like doug. u just liked him liking u.**
SnowAngel:	that's so not true! why is everybody ganging up on me?
SnowAngel:	i told zoe i was glad i moved to california, and guess what? i thoroughly and completely mean it!

ttfn

mad maddie:	**well, i talked to angela.**
zoegirl:	and?!!
mad maddie:	**she's mad as hell. ur at the top of her shit list, my friend.**
zoegirl:	oh no!!!!!
zoegirl:	i'm so stupid! stupid, stupid, stupid!
mad maddie:	**no comment**
mad maddie:	**r u ever gonna tell me what doug said to her, after she said all that about kissing him?**
zoegirl:	he got really nervous, that's all. he blurted out something like, "angela, i'm dating zoe. didn't she tell u?"
mad maddie:	**he said that out loud? that u 2 r dating?**
zoegirl:	well, yeah. and that part was totally sweet. but i doubt it made angela feel any better, since even he assumed i'd told her.
mad maddie:	**u r so screwed**
zoegirl:	i know
mad maddie:	**well, nothing i can do about it. i'm off to meet chive. laters!**

Monday, January 3, 3:30 PM E.S.T.

zoegirl:	angela, i know ur on-line. aren't u ready to talk to me yet?
Auto response from SnowAngel:	lying is lying, no matter who or where u r. and yes, zoe, this means u!
zoegirl:	angela, c'mon. don't u remember when maddie

Send   Cancel

	stonewalled us like this last year, after everything fell apart with jana? i can't believe ur doing the same thing. *please* don't be this way.
zoegirl:	anyway, don't u start school tomorrow? don't u wanna talk about it? don't u wanna obsess endlessly about what to wear?
zoegirl:	well, i'll be thinking about u. IM me!!!

Monday, January 3, 6:01 PM P.S.T.

SnowAngel:	hi, mads. i am SO not psyched to be me right now.
mad maddie:	**why? r u still feuding with zoe?**
SnowAngel:	god, who even cares?
SnowAngel:	but yeah, i guess so, if by that u mean am i still mad at her. altho what makes me even madder is that i don't WANT to be mad at her. how pathetic is that?
mad maddie:	**why don't u wanna be mad anymore?**
SnowAngel:	cuz even tho i hate her right now, i miss her 2. *scowls and kicks over trash can*
mad maddie:	**so get over yourself, u freak. u BOTH need to get over yourselves.**
SnowAngel:	whatever
SnowAngel:	so . . . tomorrow's my 1st day at El Cerrito High. i'm nervous.
mad maddie:	**ah, don't be. u'll be fine.**
SnowAngel:	what if no one likes me? what if no one talks to me?
mad maddie:	**well, there's always glendy. maybe u'll have adjoining lockers.**

Send   Cancel

SnowAngel:	oh thanks
SnowAngel:	this is so unfair that i have to be starting over in my junior year.
mad maddie:	**i agree. u belong back here with us.**
SnowAngel:	IS there still an "us"?
mad maddie:	**wtf?**
SnowAngel:	u and me and zoe. r we still an "us"?
SnowAngel:	never mind
SnowAngel:	so what should i wear tomorrow??? should i be cool and casual or sleek and sophisticated?
mad maddie:	**christ, angela, i don't know. wear whatever u want.**
SnowAngel:	when we were in the city, my mom bought me this off-the-shoulder sweater that i wear with a tank top underneath. i call it my slutwear, cuz it's pretty tight. and cuz of the shoulder thing. do u think i have good shoulders?
mad maddie:	**uh ...**
SnowAngel:	she also bought me this fuzzy white sweater with three-quarter-length sleeves. i call that one my pamela anderson sweater cuz it makes my boobs look ginormous. (well, ginormous for a 34-B)
mad maddie:	**good god**
SnowAngel:	so which should i wear??? cuz even tho my life sucks, i do wanna make a good impression.
mad maddie:	**a slutty impression?**
SnowAngel:	NO. *narrows eyes* i'm all into looking hot but classy, not like a whore.
mad maddie:	**zoe's worried that doug thinks she's a whore, btw. isn't**

Send   Cancel

	that hysterical? apparently the 2 of them got down and dirty in doug's church's basement, and things went further than zoe intended.
SnowAngel:	maddie!
SnowAngel:	stop and think for 1 single second. do u really think i wanna hear this?
mad maddie:	**ur telling me u don't?**
SnowAngel:	just how down and dirty did they get? and why were they in the church basement?
mad maddie:	**i thought u didn't wanna hear!**
SnowAngel:	i don't. *puts hands over ears*
SnowAngel:	it's just, why is he getting down and dirty with zoe instead of me?
mad maddie:	**why do u think? cuz u never acted the slightest bit interested in him until after zoe got interested. that's why this whole fight is so ridiculous.**
SnowAngel:	all i wanted was your advice on what to wear, but i can c that's not gonna happen. thanks for nothing!!!

Monday, January 3, 9:55 PM E.S.T.

mad maddie:	**ok, angela, here's something to cheer u up. it's Professor Poopypants' Name Change-O-Chart 2000. u type in your name and it spits back your new "silly" name. wanna hear yours?**
SnowAngel:	is this your peace offering?
mad maddie:	**your silly name is "stinky pizzabuns," and i'm "pinky pottybutt." i love it.**

Send   Cancel

SnowAngel:	not that i care . . . but what's zoe's?
mad maddie:	**she's got the best of all. "zsa zsa toiletsniffer."**
SnowAngel:	hmmph
SnowAngel:	should i introduce myself tomorrow as "stinky pizzabuns," do u think?
mad maddie:	**angela, that would be so awesome. u should, u totally should!**
SnowAngel:	uh . . . no
mad maddie:	**why not? it's a chance to be a whole new u!**
SnowAngel:	only i don't wanna be a whole new me! i just wanna be the normal old me, but how can i do that if no one even knows who i am?!!

Monday, January 3, 10:00 PM E.S.T.

mad maddie:	**zsa zsa, hey. i just talked to angela, and she is seriously un-stoked about her new school.**
zoegirl:	maddie! i'm so glad u IMed. but why did u call me zsa zsa?
mad maddie:	**no reason. so when r u guys gonna get over this stupid fight?**
zoegirl:	*i'm* not fighting. *she* is. and ur right, it's stupid. i left her a message on her voicemail earlier today, and i was like, "angela, c'mon. in the grand scheme of things, this is not that big a deal."
mad maddie:	**i bet that made her feel validated**
zoegirl:	i didn't mean it that way. i just meant that our friendship is stronger than this. and i've sent her tons of emails, since she won't respond to my IMs.

Send   Cancel

mad maddie:	**she's weakening. i can tell.**
zoegirl:	i dunno, but i hope so. guess i'll try her again tomorrow.

Tuesday, January 4, 4:37 PM P.S.T.

SnowAngel:	I HATE EL CERRITO HIGH SO MUCH!!!
mad maddie:	**ah, shit. what happened, a?**
SnowAngel:	they have METAL DETECTORS, maddie. everyone has to line up and walk thru this security gate, with an armed guard standing right there. it is so so so different from atlanta. it's terrible. ☹
mad maddie:	**ick, that would freak me out.**
SnowAngel:	and they've got all these stupid rules, like 4 Bs and a U.
mad maddie:	**wtf?**
SnowAngel:	it's their dress code. no breasts, bellies, backs, or butts, and no underwear. meaning, u can't have any of those things exposed. this guy in my homeroom goes, "it's like we're under control of the Taliban, man." and my homeroom teacher, whom i hate, goes, "yes, only we won't skin u alive. the word for that is 'flay,' by the way."
SnowAngel:	what a wanker
mad maddie:	**what about the ppl? u meet anyone cool?**
SnowAngel:	no. not a single person talked to me except glendy (who was wearing high-rise jeans, fyi). she glommed onto me like we were best buds, and i could c everyone looking at me and going, "L-O-S-E-R." *puts L on forehead*
mad maddie:	**u've gotta ditch the glendinizer, angela**

Send   Cancel

SnowAngel:	yeah, but how???
SnowAngel:	she gave me a little plastic Care Bear to clip onto my backpack! i tried to stuff it in the bottom compartment, and she pulled it right back out again and clipped it onto the zipper!
mad maddie:	**egad**
mad maddie:	**which care bear is it?**
SnowAngel:	Friend Bear!
SnowAngel:	SHE IS NOT MY FRIEND!!!
mad maddie:	**lose the glendinizer, that's all i can say**
SnowAngel:	gee, thanks, ur a big help
mad maddie:	**chin up, angela. this was only your 1st day—things'll get better.**
SnowAngel:	if they don't, i don't know what i'll do
mad maddie:	**well, were there any cute guys?**
SnowAngel:	no
mad maddie:	**any fun teachers?**
SnowAngel:	no
mad maddie:	**any good snack machines, for god's sake?**
SnowAngel:	they sell apples and raisins and granola bars, maddie. *bares teeth in horrid semblance of a smile*
mad maddie:	**no licorice whips? no devilishly good ding dongs?**
SnowAngel:	it's a new policy to stimulate better brain growth. freakin california!
mad maddie:	**ok, now ur depressing ME**
SnowAngel:	as if my life wasn't bad enuff, i have to read 3 chapters of biology and write a response to the 1st

Send Cancel

	20 pages of "The Heart of Darkness." *glowers* I'LL show 'em a heart of darkness.
mad maddie:	**the horror! the horror!**
SnowAngel:	i've g2g. bye!

Wednesday, January 5, 7:45 PM E.S.T.

zoegirl:	angela?
Autoresponse from SnowAngel:	"we don't need no education, we don't need no thought control!"
zoegirl:	talk to me, angela. please? i know ur on-line.
zoegirl:	fine. but things would be better if u would.
zoegirl:	and just so u know, everyone missed u at school today. especially me.

Wednesday, January 5, 4:48 PM P.S.T.

SnowAngel:	ok, i've decided to talk to u. but i'm still extremely mad.
zoegirl:	angela! hurray, hurray, hurray!
SnowAngel:	i TOLD u, i'm still mad at u.
zoegirl:	i know, i know, and i totally deserve it. and if it makes u feel any better, doug was mad at me 2. we, like, had our first fight.
SnowAngel:	how tragic—by which i mean "yay."
SnowAngel:	u fought over me?
zoegirl:	well, we didn't exactly fight, and it wasn't exactly over u. i mean, not in *that* way. but he thought i'd put u in a

Send   Cancel   129

	really bad position by not telling u about the 2 of us, and that by doing that, i put him in a really bad position.
zoegirl:	neither 1 of us meant to hurt your feelings, angela
SnowAngel:	*glares silently*
zoegirl:	please don't be mad anymore. i just got caught in my own stupidness, that's all. i really did think u didn't like him, cuz that's what u've always said.
zoegirl:	do u forgive me?
SnowAngel:	no
SnowAngel:	but i suppose if u IM, then maybe i'll IM back. and if u call my cell, i MIGHT pick up.
zoegirl:	well . . . that's a start, i guess
SnowAngel:	only i've had enuff for right now, cuz u shouldn't get off scott free after being such a jerk. so, good-bye.
zoegirl:	angela . . .
zoegirl:	r u serious? that's it, convo over?
zoegirl:	ok, fine. but IM me soon!!!

Thursday, January 6, 6:04 PM P.S.T.

SnowAngel:	hi, zoe
zoegirl:	angela, hi! wazzup?
SnowAngel:	nothing, except i guess i wanna say that i forgive u for real.
zoegirl:	u do? thank god!
SnowAngel:	my mom says it was a coping strategy to be so angry at u, that it gave me something to focus all my anger

	at. i can't control being stuck in california, but i COULD control being mad at u.
zoegirl:	huh
zoegirl:	i did kinda wonder if u were taking things out on me . . . but i also know that i really did screw up.
SnowAngel:	u got that right
zoegirl:	but i'm sorry
SnowAngel:	*deep, cleansing breath* and i forgive u
SnowAngel:	so now u have to tell me about him, since u didn't for all this time.
zoegirl:	who, doug?
SnowAngel:	no, george bush. of course doug!!!
zoegirl:	well . . . he's wonderful. he's funny and he's sweet and he's got a poster of kermit the frog in his room.
zoegirl:	r u sure u want to hear this?
SnowAngel:	no, turns out i don't
SnowAngel:	just tell me 1 thing. do u honestly like him? like, a lot?
zoegirl:	yeah . . . i do.
SnowAngel:	why? i'm not being a brat, i really wanna know.
zoegirl:	oh, angela
zoegirl:	i like him cuz when we talk, it feels real. like, last nite we sat on the floor of the den and watched this candle burn down, and we talked about all kinds of things—our families, what we wanna do when we're older, what we believe in terms of God.
zoegirl:	it's just so rare to find someone—a guy!—who gets me, u know? who doesn't make me feel fake when i say what i'm honestly thinking.

131

SnowAngel:	yeah, i can c that
zoegirl:	altho then it was weird when we finally stopped talking and it was time for him to go. he kept jingling his keys, but he wouldn't get up from the sofa and walk out the door. cuz i guess he was . . . thinking we should fool around.
SnowAngel:	what???
zoegirl:	never mind, that just slipped out. i didn't mean to bring up a touchy subject.
SnowAngel:	it's 2 late now. tell me!
zoegirl:	r u sure?
SnowAngel:	if u don't, it will just make things worse.
zoegirl:	well, on our 1st date we kinda fooled around, ok? more than we should have, maybe. only why do i feel like that, like we *shouldn't* have? tons of ppl fool around. maddie fools around all the time. so if doug and i wanna fool around, we should, right?
SnowAngel:	is this my little zoe, all grown up? should i be putting on my mom's "Fiddler on the Roof" cd? *strikes melancholy pose* "Is this the little girl I carried? Is this the little boy at play? I don't remember growing older. When did they?"
zoegirl:	r u making fun of me?
SnowAngel:	"Sunrise, sunset. Sunrise, sunset. Swiftly flow the days!"
zoegirl:	stop singing!!!!!!!
SnowAngel:	ok, let's recap. u got down and dirty on your 1st date, and last nite doug wanted an instant replay. did u give him one or not?

Send   Cancel

zoegirl:	*not* we kissed, but i didn't let it go further than that. finally i said, "doug, we have to get some sleep. u have to go." he didn't take the hint, so i pulled him up and propelled him to the door and very unsubtly pushed him toward his car.
zoegirl:	i'm worried he thought i was being a jerk.
SnowAngel:	yeah, he probably did
SnowAngel:	jk
zoegirl:	i didn't know it would be this complicated. the physical stuff, i mean.
SnowAngel:	just remember that as much as it pains me to say it, it really is ok to fool around or kiss or whatever u wanna call it. bodies r meant to do that.
zoegirl:	i know
SnowAngel:	and there's a difference b/w fooling around and hooking up.
SnowAngel:	ur not maddie, zoe. don't worry.
zoegirl:	ouch
zoegirl:	but thanks. i know this can't be the easiest thing for u to talk about.
SnowAngel:	get real. what kind of twisted friend would freak out over a guy she'd never even gone out with???
SnowAngel:	anyway, that's what i'm here for, even if i AM 3,000 miles away.

Thursday, January 6, 9:32 PM E.S.T.

zoegirl:	wait! we forgot to talk about U! do u wanna tell me about your new school?

Send   Cancel

SnowAngel: nah, i'm pretty wiped. i'm just glad things r good b/w us.

zoegirl: me 2. nite!

Friday, January 7, 6:50 PM E.S.T.

mad maddie: u know what i hate? ppl who hate everyone. ppl who walk around so wrapped up in their own bullshit that they can't possibly imagine that everyone else might NOT be as fake as they wanna think they r.

SnowAngel: and hello to u 2. what r u going on about?

mad maddie: just cuz i don't wear all black and a studded collar, that makes me a sell-out? that automatically implies that i worship jessica simpson?

SnowAngel: i like jessica simpson. she's ditzy, but she seems sweet.

mad maddie: don't tell katie thompson and her minions that. they were trolling the halls today in their black eyeliner and their "wacky" clothes, and i was like, "god, i'm sick of school already, and i've only been back 3 days." the katies think they're so DIFFERENT, but they can only be different in a group. have u noticed?

SnowAngel: i did back in the good old days, yes. but in case u've forgotten, katie and i no longer live in the same state.

mad maddie: i know that. DER.

mad maddie: i just mean that if ur gonna be different, u should be different for real, not cuz of some bullshit desire to be

134

different. like—well, hold on. chive says it better than me. here, this is from his deadjournal:

Chet Baker is *the man*. Never learned to read music, because he heard the music in his soul. Lived hard and fast, because that's what living is for. He lost his teeth in a street fight, but still he was the best jazz trumpet player this world has seen. The prince of cool.

Check it out, from "Chet Baker's Unsung Swan Song" by David Wilcox:

My old addiction
Makes me crave only what is best,
Like these just this morning song birds
Craving upward from the nest.

mad maddie:	**doesn't that say it all?**
SnowAngel:	i don't get it. who's chet baker?
mad maddie:	**just the best jazz trumpet player ever. it says it right there.**
SnowAngel:	what's the bit about the birds craving upward from the nest? is it poetry?
mad maddie:	**it's a SONG by david wilcox. don't u know who david wilcox is?**
SnowAngel:	no
SnowAngel:	did U, pre-chive?
mad maddie:	**it's about how chet b. died by falling out of a hotel window. he was wasted, apparently. hence, like a bird leaning out of its nest.**

Send   Cancel   135

SnowAngel:	a bird that was wasted?
mad maddie:	**the point is that chet baker lived life on his own terms, unlike katie thompson. he took risks. he was unpredictable.**
SnowAngel:	u don't have to be wasted to be unpredictable. i'm not a goth girl OR a wastoid, and I'M unpredictable.
mad maddie:	**U? hahahahahaha**
mad maddie:	**i love u, angela, but ur as predictable as they come. type in "16-year-old girl" and out pops "angela silver."**
SnowAngel:	excuse me? name ONE thing about me that's predictable!
mad maddie:	**uh, let's c. your chad michael murray obsession? your need to shop? and let's not forget the fight ur having with zoe, which is over the most predictable thing in the world—a guy.**
SnowAngel:	what fight? we worked things out.
mad maddie:	**come again?**
SnowAngel:	i still think she handled everything completely wrong . . . but MAYBE i shouldn't have made such a case out of her hanging out with doug. maybe i sorta knew that she liked him all along.
mad maddie:	**oh**
mad maddie:	**that doesn't make it ok, tho. she LIED to u.**
SnowAngel:	i know she did
mad maddie:	**more than once, i might add.**
SnowAngel:	what's your point? do u not want me to forgive her?
mad maddie:	**no, i do. of course i do.**
SnowAngel:	good, cuz i did

Send   Cancel

SnowAngel:	and u wanna know what's weird? it was a total power trip to let her off the hook. i didn't know it was gonna be, but it was. it was such a role reversal—the great zoe messing up!
SnowAngel:	does that make any sense?
mad maddie:	**u got to be the magnanimous one. u got to choose whether to let her live or die.**
SnowAngel:	yeah. i'm not saying i'm glad it happened . . . but part of me liked having her grovel.
mad maddie:	**i can totally understand**
SnowAngel:	plus, what else was i supposed to do?
SnowAngel:	she's my zoe, just like ur my maddie. i can't live w/o either of u.
mad maddie:	**lucky for u, u don't have to.**
SnowAngel:	which is good, cuz now i won't have to get wasted and fall out a hotel window.
mad maddie:	**haha, very funny!**

Saturday, January 8, 11:45 AM E.S.T.

zoegirl:	finally ur up! geez, i thought maddie was bad, but even maddie's up by noon.
SnowAngel:	*rubs sleep from eyes* it's not noon here, zoe. we're 3 hours earlier, remember?
zoegirl:	oh yeah, i forgot
zoegirl:	so that makes it . . . 8:45? wow, ur up early.
SnowAngel:	*smiles wanly*
zoegirl:	so what's going on? u have any big plans for tonite?

SnowAngel:	no, cuz i have no friends, cuz apparently i suck.
zoegirl:	what about glendy?
SnowAngel:	haha. glendy is WORSE than no friends.
SnowAngel:	yesterday she cornered me at lunch and made me go to the bathroom with her. she needed me to run water in the sink while she . . . did her business. what a baby!
zoegirl:	why run water?
zoegirl:	oh, to cover the sounds?
SnowAngel:	she doesn't want anyone to hear her peeing. isn't that something ur supposed to be over by the time ur 16? i was like, "we ALL do it, glendy. every single 1 of us pees, even mother teresa."
zoegirl:	i have a hard time peeing around other ppl 2, tho. in my head i'm like, "just pee, just pee!" but sometimes my body refuses to cooperate.
zoegirl:	oh god. does that mean i'm repressed?
SnowAngel:	huh?
zoegirl:	maddie thinks i am. she says i'm a prude.
SnowAngel:	no offense, but compared to maddie, anyone would be a prude
SnowAngel:	oops *claps hand over mouth*
zoegirl:	sometimes i worry she's right, tho. like with doug, i still get nervous about all the body stuff. i can never just let go and enjoy it, not all the way.
zoegirl:	am i allowed to talk to u about this? i don't wanna make u feel bad.
SnowAngel:	the only time u make me feel bad is when u say things like "i don't wanna make u feel bad."

Send   Cancel

138

SnowAngel:	so when u say u can't just let go and enjoy it . . . does that mean things have been progressing?
zoegirl:	well, doug wants them 2. i keep kind of redirecting him.
SnowAngel:	ahhh, redirecting him. that's a good way to put it.
zoegirl:	why do i have to be this way? it's like i'm stuck in my stupid head, thinking, "crap, did i shave? do i smell? r my breasts 2 small? is my butt 2 big?"
SnowAngel:	zoe, your butt is NOT 2 big. if your butt is 2 big, then the rest of us should jump over a cliff and be done with it.
zoegirl:	and even worse . . .
zoegirl:	never mind. i don't wanna say.
SnowAngel:	SAY IT
zoegirl:	no, cuz then u'll *really* think i'm a prude!
SnowAngel:	u don't like to pee around him?
zoegirl:	angela! as if.
SnowAngel:	then what?
zoegirl:	it doesn't have to do with peeing noises, it has to do with . . . other noises.
SnowAngel:	other noises? OHHH, like body noises, u mean? like slurps and squelches?
zoegirl:	ok, please let's not put names on them. i'm totally turning bright red.
zoegirl:	but yeah, *those noises*
zoegirl:	i wanna get over it, i really do. i wanna let go and let whatever happens happen. but i can't!
SnowAngel:	wait a minute. if ur worried about noises, then u guys must have gone pretty far . . .

Send   Cancel

139

zoegirl:	below the shirt, below the underwear. *but just barely*
SnowAngel:	his or yours?
zoegirl:	uh, both?
SnowAngel:	holy cats!
SnowAngel:	zoe, u r not a prude, ok? in fact i'd say ur turning into a sex guru. shit, girl, ur gonna outpace us all! ☺

Saturday, January 8, 3:33 PM E.S.T.

mad maddie:	**it is a mistake to wear low-riders if u have a big ass. i am not saying this to be mean, but because it is the truth.**
zoegirl:	oh, great! i just asked angela straight out if i have a big butt, and she said no!
mad maddie:	**U? ur a size 2, zoe.**
mad maddie:	**the ass in question is margo pedersen's. she was working at java joe's when i went by for a latte, and she had to lean over to get the milk. nuff said.**
zoegirl:	oh
mad maddie:	**u gonna c doug tonite?**
zoegirl:	yeah, at work. and we'll probably do something afterward.
mad maddie:	**ooh-la-la. give him a kissy for me!**

Sunday, January 9, 12:50 PM E.S.T.

zoegirl:	hey, angela. i have something i wanna tell u, but i'm not sure i should, only i really want to cuz it's making me all smiley inside. can i tell u, or will it secretly make u sad?

Send   Cancel

SnowAngel:	what r u blithering about? does this have to do with doug?
zoegirl:	yeah, and i can't tell maddie cuz she'd make fun of me. so can i tell u, or would u rather i not?
SnowAngel:	OMG, DID U HAVE SEX??????
zoegirl:	angela, shhhhh!
SnowAngel:	what, u think everyone in cyberland can hear?
SnowAngel:	SO DID U????
zoegirl:	no! of course not!
SnowAngel:	darn
SnowAngel:	altho not really cuz i don't think i'm actually ready for that
zoegirl:	*ur* not ready? what about *me*?
SnowAngel:	not everything is about U, zoe
SnowAngel:	do u remember saying that to me, back when u 1st started lying? now u know what it feels like!
zoegirl:	why r u snapping at me? r u in a bad mood?
zoegirl:	talking to u isn't as fun as i thought it was gonna be.
SnowAngel:	i'm sorry, i'm sorry *drops to knees and hugs friend's legs*
SnowAngel:	PLEASE tell me. i'll stop being obnoxious, i promise.
zoegirl:	well . . . now it doesn't even seem like a big deal anymore. only, it is.
zoegirl:	he wrote a poem for me—isn't that sweet?
SnowAngel:	awww! can i read it?
zoegirl:	yes, cuz he posted it on poetry.com, which means that *anyone* can read it. i think that's so cool, cuz it means

	he's not, like, hiding it or anything. he wants the whole world to know.
SnowAngel:	should i go to the site right now?
zoegirl:	no, i'll paste it in. but later u can visit the site and c for yourself how official it looks.
zoegirl:	here it is. it's called "Miraculous Thing."

Miraculous Thing

Today all of the news is good news.
This morning a robin
lands on my porch
and beeps her hip hop
until dark.
I can't help tapping my foot.
I take her by the wing
and we dance into flight.
It is you, Zoe,
lifting me higher and higher
into the starry night
that reminds me
of your eyes and the sparkling
touch of your skin.
I may never sleep again.

zoegirl:	isn't it beautiful and wonderful and perfect??? or do i just think so cuz it's about me?
SnowAngel:	it's different from the poem he read at the poetry slam last year, that's for sure. that 1 was about dirty underwear.

Send   Cancel

zoegirl:	no one's ever written me a poem before.
SnowAngel:	no one's written me 1 either.
SnowAngel:	ur lucky, zo
zoegirl:	i know. thanks for being so cool about it.
zoegirl:	but mum's the word when it comes to maddie, ok?
SnowAngel:	🙂
SnowAngel:	bye!

Sunday, January 9, 2:24 PM E.S.T.

mad maddie:	hey, a-boogie. chumley the psycho kitty scratched the hell out of my leg, and now i have 3 long gashes on my thigh. they look really cool.
mad maddie:	is that sick, that i like the look of pain?
SnowAngel:	yes
mad maddie:	tell me ur not the same, tho. like when u get a bruise, don't u feel tough?
SnowAngel:	i've always secretly wanted a black eye, to tell the truth
mad maddie:	YES! that's exactly what i mean!
SnowAngel:	we r sick little freaks, aren't we?
mad maddie:	never said we weren't
mad maddie:	so wassup?
SnowAngel:	nothing much. i IMed with zo earlier—she's doing well.
mad maddie:	oh yeah?
SnowAngel:	in fact i shouldn't tell u this, but i'm going to anyway. 🙂
SnowAngel:	doug wrote her a poem.

Send   Cancel

mad maddie:	**oh good lord**
SnowAngel:	it's called "miraculous thing."
mad maddie:	**"miraculous thing"? what, now zoe's a bona fide miracle?**
SnowAngel:	it's sweet, tho. it really is. it's posted under his name on www.poetry.com if u wanna check it out.
mad maddie:	**heck yeah, i'm gonna pull it up right now.**
SnowAngel:	did u find it? is it there?
mad maddie:	**jesus, angela. "i take her by the wing and we dance into flight"??? who IS this freak?**
SnowAngel:	*chortle chortle*
SnowAngel:	i take it chive hasn't written U any love poems . . .
mad maddie:	**NO, thank god**
SnowAngel:	doug must really like her a lot. *deflates a little, like a balloon* i'm embarrassed to say it, but it makes me the TINIEST bit jealous.
mad maddie:	**why??? cuz u wanna be compared to a robin?**
SnowAngel:	ha, i knew u'd make me feel better. ☺
SnowAngel:	seriously, tho, u can't tell zoe i told u.
mad maddie:	**excuse me, but it's on the world wide web. it's fair game.**
SnowAngel:	i know, but don't mention it anyway.
mad maddie:	**she should have told me. i hate it when she keeps secrets.**
mad maddie:	**but don't worry, i know how to keep my mouth shut!**

Send   Cancel

Monday, January 10, 8:36 PM E.S.T.

mad maddie:	**hey, zo. have u noticed mary kate's new way of talking? it's driving me up the wall.**
zoegirl:	what's she doing?
mad maddie:	**she, like, makes all her vowels long, like "agane" instead of "again." and she calls her mom "mum." i wanna vomit every time she opens her mouth.**
zoegirl:	i don't get it. is she trying to be British?
mad maddie:	**god only knows. it is nauseatingly pretentious.**
mad maddie:	**anywayz, that's all i wanted to say. i'm off to meet chive at the awful waffle.**
zoegirl:	wait! ur leaving? that's it?
mad maddie:	**yeah, so?**
zoegirl:	nothing, it's just that we haven't talked in forever.
mad maddie:	**that's cuz u've been busy with doug**
zoegirl:	and *u've* been busy with chive
mad maddie:	**blah blah blah. anywayz, i IMed u on saturday, or have u forgotten?**
zoegirl:	but that was super-short. it was like a fake IM. like u thought, "ooo, better IM zoe," only u didn't actually *tell* me anything.
mad maddie:	**whereas u, on the other hand, make it a point to tell me everything?**
zoegirl:	huh? what's that supposed to mean?
mad maddie:	**i've gtg, i'm supposed to be there in 15 minutes.**
zoegirl:	then IM me when u get back.
mad maddie:	**it'll probably be late, but fine. IF ur even on-line!**

Tuesday, January 11, 11:39 PM E.S.T.

mad maddie:	**zo-ster! u R up!**
zoegirl:	maddie, hi!
mad maddie:	**oh yeah? how high r u?**
zoegirl:	???
zoegirl:	i'm so glad u IMed—i've been staying on-line just in case. so what'd u do? did u have fun?
mad maddie:	**mmmm, waffles. i could eat 5 more right now. and chive played the jukebox and the jukebox played him. hehehehe.**
zoegirl:	what do u mean, the jukebox played him?
mad maddie:	**who knows? i mean what i say and i say what i mean.**
mad maddie:	**aren't jukeboxes COOL, tho? i mean, it's like back in the good ol days. a blast from the last.**
zoegirl:	i think u mean a blast from the *past*
mad maddie:	**oh man, do u ever feel like your teeth r 2 sharp? my teeth r really, really sharp.**
zoegirl:	what r u talking about? r u ok, maddie?
mad maddie:	**special lady! waitin on me at the waffle house. she's amazin! calling all those orders out. special lady!**
zoegirl:	omg, r u stoned?!
mad maddie:	**hey, i resemble that remark! hehehehehe**
zoegirl:	i'm serious. r u stoned?
mad maddie:	**it's a song from the waffle house jukebox. am i chive's special lady? i wanna be chive's special lady.**
mad maddie:	**and no, i'm not stoned. the word i could easily write to show u that i'm not would be trilogy. or in stone in frye**

Send   Cancel

	in capsula. or i could go to bed even tho i know i'll be in big trouble.
zoegirl:	why r u gonna be in trouble?
mad maddie:	**cuz the moms thought that 2, ya know. about being stoned.**
mad maddie:	**oh man, i just realized something! u and the moms, ur like twins! u were separated at birth!**
zoegirl:	maddie, i don't c the point in talking to u right now unless ur gonna start acting normal.
mad maddie:	**define normal. what's normal, zoe? r U normal?**
zoegirl:	bye, mads. ur making me feel really sad.
mad maddie:	**sad mad glad. how weird that they all rhyme.**
mad maddie:	**u should go eat a waffle! u can't be sad if u eat a waffle!!!**

Wednesday, January 12, 10:34 AM E.S.T.

zoegirl:	thank god, angela. i'm so glad ur on-line. what time is it there, like 7:30 in the morning?
SnowAngel:	yeah, and glendy's dad is gonna be here to pick me up any minute. what about u? why aren't u in school?
zoegirl:	i am. i'm IMing from the media center.
zoegirl:	angela, maddie IMed me last nite when she was stoned. it was *awful*
SnowAngel:	she was stoned? how could u tell?
zoegirl:	it was impossible not to. she kept going on about these random things and none of her sentences made sense and it was just scary. it's like she wasn't even herself.
SnowAngel:	yikes

147

zoegirl:	i know. it's 1 thing to know that she's become this big pothead, but it's another to c it in action. i didn't like it, angela.
SnowAngel:	did u tell her that?
zoegirl:	no, cuz there was no point. she was *stoned*
SnowAngel:	well, r u gonna tell her today?
zoegirl:	i saw her before homeroom, and i just played it cool. but she had to have known that something was up.
SnowAngel:	not necessarily. ppl c what they wanna c.
SnowAngel:	crap, mr. boss just pulled up in front of our apartment. TELL HER, ZOE!

Wednesday, January 12, 8:44 PM E.S.T.

zoegirl:	hi, maddie. i have to tell u something.
mad maddie:	**yeah, wazzup? did u catch mary kate's brit-speak today?**
zoegirl:	it's not about mary kate. it's about u.
mad maddie:	**meaning?**
zoegirl:	meaning that i'm worried about u. it's been like this unspoken thing between us—even tho i've noticed u feel quite comfortable telling *angela* about it—but i don't wanna shove it under the rug anymore.
mad maddie:	**shove what under the rug?**
zoegirl:	think about it: with the whole doug thing, i didn't tell angela cuz i didn't wanna upset her, and of course that just made everything worse.
zoegirl:	maybe friends *have* to upset each other once in a while. maybe that's what being a real friend means.

Send   Cancel

mad maddie:	is this about last nite? i was just messing with u, u know that.
zoegirl:	no, u weren't. u were . . . freaky, maddie.
zoegirl:	it scared me.
mad maddie:	oh please. ur such an old woman.
zoegirl:	i'm an old woman cuz i don't want u smoking pot?
zoegirl:	u weren't U, maddie. u could hardly string 3 words together.
mad maddie:	zoe, chill. THIS is why i never bring it up with u.
zoegirl:	no, u never bring it up with me cuz u don't want anyone pointing out that it's wrong!
mad maddie:	it's "wrong"? smoking pot is "wrong"? when did U get to be the morality police?
zoegirl:	it's wrong cuz it's bad for u—and u know it
mad maddie:	says who?
mad maddie:	u may not like the choices i make, but at least i'm LIVING. at least i won't look back at my life when i'm 100 years old and say, "i was too afraid to try that and i was too afraid to try that."
zoegirl:	cuz u won't have any brain cells left, that's why
mad maddie:	omg. maybe ur happy leading your boring safe life, but i'm not taking that route. i refuse to numb out.
zoegirl:	which is why u get stoned and drunk? cuz u don't wanna numb yourself out?
mad maddie:	pot AMPLIFIES the experience, zoe
mad maddie:	forget it. u've never tried it, so how can u even talk?
zoegirl:	cuz i'm not stupid. cuz i like my brain in full working order, thank u very much. and cuz i'm not about to get high just to impress a guy who thinks life is 1 big party.

Send   Cancel

149

mad maddie:	**god, ur self-righteous**
zoegirl:	u don't have to get drunk or smoke pot in order to live life to the fullest, maddie.
mad maddie:	**oh yeah? what DO u have to do? study really hard? be a good little girl and do everything everyone tells u to do?**
zoegirl:	ur trying to make this about me, but it's not
mad maddie:	**name 1 thing u've done recently that pushed u out of your comfort zone, that made your heart pound. and u can't say fooling around with doug, cuz that doesn't count.**
mad maddie:	**anywayz, u can't even give yourself fully over to that, can u? tell me that's not incredibly pathetic.**
zoegirl:	i can't believe u said that
zoegirl:	that is so not true
mad maddie:	**it's not?**
zoegirl:	well it's not as pathetic as fooling around with someone else's boyfriend! it's not as pathetic as pretending that's the way u want it when really u wish he was yours!
mad maddie:	**exsqueeze me?**
zoegirl:	"i want to be chive's special lady." that's what u said last nite.
mad maddie:	**i did NOT**
zoegirl:	those were your very words—go back and look! and i know that's why ur smoking so much, to make yourself stand out from whitney. but whitney's the 1 he's with, isn't she?
mad maddie:	**so?**
zoegirl:	so ur lying to yourself, maddie!

Send   Cancel

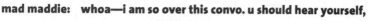

mad maddie:	**whoa—i am so over this convo. u should hear yourself, man. u r majorly worked up.**
zoegirl:	don't tell me i'm not living my life fully. don't tell me that i'm the 1 with the problem.
mad maddie:	**"most men lead lives of quiet desperation." that's u in a nutshell.**
zoegirl:	omg. show off for chive, not me.
zoegirl:	why r we even friends, maddie?
mad maddie:	**WHAT?**
zoegirl:	i'm serious. why r we even friends? i'm not trying to be mean—i'm honestly wondering. we both get along great with angela, and when we're all 3 together, everything's fine. but we're not all 3 together. and when it's just the 2 of us, everything seems to fall apart.
mad maddie:	**don't say that. that's not true.**
zoegirl:	i don't *not* want to be friends.
zoegirl:	but it's like, everything gets blown up between us. everything gets rubbed the wrong way.
mad maddie:	**not always. not even usually.**
zoegirl:	lots, tho
mad maddie:	**i just think that if ur gonna point all this blame at me, then u have to look at yourself, 2. ur not perfect, zoe.**
zoegirl:	i never said i was
mad maddie:	**well u sure act like it sometimes!**

Thursday, January 13, 10:35 PM E.S.T.

mad maddie:	**hey, a. did u hear about the big blowout? i'm sure u did.**

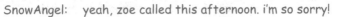

SnowAngel:	yeah, zoe called this afternoon. i'm so sorry!
mad maddie:	**she drives me up the wall. u should have heard how self-righteous she was being.**
SnowAngel:	well like i said, i'm sorry.
SnowAngel:	but i kinda need to tell u that i don't entirely disagree with her. i mean, i've been worried about u 2. *shies back to avoid wrath*
mad maddie:	**u don't need to be. god.**
mad maddie:	**anywayz, the moms had already been riding me before zoe IMed. i didn't tell zoe, but that's part of why i jumped all over her.**
SnowAngel:	riding u about what?
mad maddie:	**the same thing zoe was, my "alleged" poor decision-making skills. she was all, "ur not smoking marijuana, r u maddie?"**
mad maddie:	**only she pronounced it mare-uh-joo-wah-nah. she's so lame.**
SnowAngel:	shit, maddie, does she KNOW?
mad maddie:	**she has her suspicions, which i neither confirmed nor denied.**
mad maddie:	**actually, i denied the hell out of them. but where does the moms get the right to come down on me? she and dad r the worst role models ever. and has SHE smoked pot? yes, she has. last nite she told me that she and the dads smoked "mare-uh-joo-wah-nah" at some party when i was a kid, and it almost cost her her marriage.**
SnowAngel:	whoa, your MOM smoked pot? your parents r so cool.
SnowAngel:	why did it almost cost her her marriage?
mad maddie:	**she got all flirty with some other guy or something. i'm**

Send   Cancel

	sure she was blowing it out of proportion. it was like her little cautionary tale to scare me straight.
mad maddie:	**so the point is that the moms had laid all that on me— very serious and "this is your life, maddie"—and then zoe IMed me and gave me the exact same lecture, only worse. can u c why i got upset?**
SnowAngel:	i guess
mad maddie:	**AND i somehow managed to lose my wallet at the waffle house, which is a major drag. i didn't have much money, but i did have my license in it. aaargh.**
mad maddie:	**anywayz, i just wanted to explain the whole story to u. i don't want everyone hating me.**
SnowAngel:	nobody hates u, maddie. we could NEVER hate u.
mad maddie:	**u wanna know what's weird? and i could never ever tell zoe, so u better not either.**
SnowAngel:	what?
mad maddie:	**contrary to popular opinion, i don't actually LOVE getting stoned.**
SnowAngel:	i know, cuz it burns
mad maddie:	**yeah, there's that. but it also just kinda ... makes things icky.**
SnowAngel:	like how?
mad maddie:	**it changes things. it's like everyone gets all distorted, and i can c what they're really thinking, and i don't like it. i can c how desperate we all r, cuz the layers get peeled off, and we're just these naked bundles of need.**
SnowAngel:	er, i'm not exactly following
mad maddie:	**like, ok, tuesday nite at the waffle house? we're all crammed into this booth, and whenever brannen says**

Send   Cancel

something, he looks at me in this overly eager way. only i'm 2 busy looking at chive, who's 2 busy looking at whitney . . .

mad maddie: ugh. i guess i can't explain it.

SnowAngel: why do u do it, then? get stoned?

mad maddie: i dunno. cuz sometimes it's bad, but it can also be hilarious. like mad-laffing hilarity, where u just go on and on and on and u don't even know what set u off. that part's awesome.

SnowAngel: but we do that without pot, like when zoe was trying to learn how to drive stick shift and she kept rolling down the hill. remember?

mad maddie: yeah, i know

SnowAngel: we USED to have mad-laffing hilarity, that is. we haven't for a long time.

mad maddie: i hear u

SnowAngel: tell me something funny. tell me something to make me laff.

mad maddie: um . . . i can't think of anything

mad maddie: wait, i know. today in english, mariah rath goes, "mr. phelps, it is SO cold in here. aren't u cold?" and mr. phelps goes, "noooo, i'm a little teacup."

SnowAngel: ???

mad maddie: u know, from that song. "i'm a little teacup, short and stout. here is my handle, here is my spout."

SnowAngel: it's teaPOT, not teacup

SnowAngel: and that's not very funny

mad maddie: it was at the time. mr. phelps is such a dork, u can't help but love him.

Send   Cancel

SnowAngel:	*blinks non-committally*
mad maddie:	**ah, angela. i'm outta here, ok? c yas!**

Friday, January 14, 7:02 PM P.S.T.

SnowAngel:	zoe, why do ppl wear nude-colored hose? i really don't understand.
zoegirl:	um, cuz they think they look good?
SnowAngel:	but they don't. they never do.
SnowAngel:	glendy wore nude-colored hose today, with open-toed white leather sandals, no less. in january!!!
zoegirl:	ooo, that's bad
SnowAngel:	this morning she was all worked up about a bit of blueberry in her teeth that a guy she likes may or may not have seen, and i was like, "girl, u have bigger things to worry about."
zoegirl:	like nude-colored hose?
SnowAngel:	exactly
zoegirl:	poor thing
SnowAngel:	poor thing my foot!
SnowAngel:	she invited me to spend the nite tomorrow nite, can u believe it? i politely declined, and she goes, "oh, would tonite be better? cuz we can do tonite, no problem." i told her i couldn't do that either, cuz mom wants me to get my room put together so that it doesn't look like i'm living in a refugee camp. so glendy goes, "well, i'll come help u. i know! i know! we can get matching comforters!!!"
zoegirl:	she did not

SnowAngel:	she DID, zoe. and i've seen her comforter—it's this crappy polyester deal with dolphins all over it.
zoegirl:	so is she gonna come help u decorate?
SnowAngel:	r u kidding? glendy may have this illusion that we're friends, but we're not. i already have my friends, thank u very much.
SnowAngel:	*droops* they're just not with me.
zoegirl:	oh, angela. i wish i were there to help u decorate.
SnowAngel:	i don't wanna decorate. i don't even care about decorating.
zoegirl:	so what did u say to glendy?
SnowAngel:	i said, "thanks so much for offering, but how boring that would be for u." and she said, "no, i want to, really!" and i said, "that is SO sweet, but i'm not roping anyone in to do my work." i just kept smiling and not backing down no matter what she said.
zoegirl:	ack. it kinda makes me feel sorry for her.
SnowAngel:	don't u DARE feel sorry for her. she's snivelly.
SnowAngel:	after she finally got it thru her skull that i wasn't gonna invite her over, she got all pouty and said, "i thought southern girls were supposed to be nice." i looked at her like, "what drug r u on?" and she quickly said, "just kidding."
zoegirl:	hey now, southern girls R nice
SnowAngel:	the point was, she needed to frickin take the hint
SnowAngel:	that pouty crap might work with mr. boss, but not with me. *wipes her hands of the annoying glendy*
zoegirl:	u crack me up
SnowAngel:	so have u smoothed things out with maddie yet?

Send   Cancel

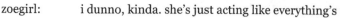

zoegirl:	i dunno, kinda. she's just acting like everything's normal, only everything *isn't* normal, so it feels depressing and wrong.
SnowAngel:	believe me, i know all about depressing and wrong.
SnowAngel:	grrr—i'm gonna go stick my head in the toaster oven. bye!

Monday, January 17, 12:23 PM E.S.T.

mad maddie:	**oh, martin luther king junior, i thank u for this day of rest. for without u, i would be in SPANISH right now instead of the lovely java joe's, sipping my delicious chai.**
SnowAngel:	i'm jealous. i want a chai!
mad maddie:	**here, i'll pour some thru the computer. gurgle, slurple, gack.**
SnowAngel:	*smacks lips* mmm, thanx. only now my keyboard's all sticky.
SnowAngel:	so zoe says ur being all fakey around her. r u?
mad maddie:	**what?!**
mad maddie:	**no, i'm not being fakey. how annoying that she would say that.**
SnowAngel:	she says ur acting normal, but that things AREN'T normal.
mad maddie:	**if things aren't normal, it's cuz of her. she thinks i'm 2 wild, but the reality is, she's 2 much of a wimp. she's like a timid little mouse. she's afraid to live in the real world.**
SnowAngel:	ohhhh, i c
SnowAngel:	and it's your job to make her realize this?

Send   Cancel

mad maddie:	**i never said that**
mad maddie:	**only . . . yeah! ur brilliant, angela. maybe it is!**
SnowAngel:	maybe it is what? now i'm confused.
SnowAngel:	maddie?
SnowAngel:	come back and explain what ur talking about!!!

Tuesday, January 18, 6:40 PM E.S.T.

mad maddie:	**hey, zo. wazzup?**
zoegirl:	nothing much. u?
mad maddie:	**nothin. i thought of u today in english, tho.**
zoegirl:	oh yeah? why?
mad maddie:	**cuz of something the little baptist girl said.**
zoegirl:	what little baptist girl?
mad maddie:	**she was talking really loudly to her friend with the mole, and out of her mouth came, "no way! shut the hell up!" it was very unexpected.**
zoegirl:	r u talking about alicia arnold? u shouldn't call her the "little baptist girl."
mad maddie:	**that's true. she's more of a big baptist girl, isn't she? anywayz, the whole class heard and she turned bright red. and then she said, "it's your fault, mr. phelps. i picked it up from u, and now it's stuck in my brain!"**
zoegirl:	mr. phelps says "shut the hell up"?
mad maddie:	**in a jokey way. like, he'll look at us at the beginning of class and say, "all right, all right, shut the hell up. who's finished chapter 12 of 'Things Fall Apart'?" but now he says he'll quit on account of corrupting the big baptist girl.**

158

zoegirl:	maddie, u r bad
zoegirl:	but why in the world did that make u think of me?
mad maddie:	**cuz i started wondering, have U ever said "shut the hell up"? if alicia arnold can, then surely u can 2. i give u permission.**
zoegirl:	haha
mad maddie:	**no, seriously. i think it would be good for you. ur so afraid of screwing up, but it IS ok to break a rule or 2 every once in a while. maybe if u did, u wouldn't be such a chickenshit.**
zoegirl:	i'm a *chickenshit*?
mad maddie:	**um, yeah. just think about the whole angela/doug mess: if u weren't so wimpy, u would have told her in the 1st place. u said it yourself.**
zoegirl:	u can't use that as an example. it's over and done with.
mad maddie:	**but ur still a chickenshit—that's my point.**
zoegirl:	i am not a chickenshit. stop saying that.
mad maddie:	**then prove me wrong. pick anyone—anyone u want, as long as it's not me or angela—and tell them to shut the hell up. i dare u.**
zoegirl:	that's the stupidest thing i've ever heard.
mad maddie:	**why, cuz ur scared?**
zoegirl:	no, cuz it's *stupid*
mad maddie:	**that proves it—ur a chickenshit!**

Tuesday, January 18, 6:55 PM E.S.T.

mad maddie:	**hey, a. i totally called zoe on her bullshit! it was hilarious.**
SnowAngel:	it was? what'd u do?

Send   Cancel

mad maddie:	**i dared her to tell someone to shut the hell up. can u imagine those words ever coming out of zoe's mouth?**
mad maddie:	**i was like, "c! u criticize me for being willing to take risks, but isn't that better than being the perpetual good girl, locked in your land of repression?"**
SnowAngel:	whatever, mads. u sound a little wacko 2 me.
mad maddie:	**nah, i'm just gloating. u should have heard how defensive she got—hahahahaha!**
SnowAngel:	u shouldn't gloat about your friends. u should love them. and when they're feeling defensive, or left out, or just lonely, then u should do whatever u can to make them feel better. u should only want what's best for them!
mad maddie:	**huh?**
mad maddie:	**well, this IS what's best for her—to realize she's flawed just like the rest of us.**
mad maddie:	**and now, off for a celebratory glass of nestle quik. l8rs!**

Wednesday, January 19, 5:05 PM E.S.T.

zoegirl:	ok, mads, i did it. r u happy?
mad maddie:	**u did what?**
mad maddie:	**no u didn't. ur lying.**
zoegirl:	i'm not. i told chase dickinson to shut the hell up!
mad maddie:	**bullshit**
zoegirl:	he was talking to kurt manheim in french about all kinds of disgusting stuff, that's what started it. he was all, "my rep's getting pathetic cuz i haven't had sex in over a month," and

Send   Cancel

	"that's why i need a girlfriend, someone older who can teach me stuff. someone who'll give me head."
mad maddie:	**he said all this in french?**
zoegirl:	not *in* french, as in parlez vous francais. but right there in the middle of class, yeah. he sits behind me.
mad maddie:	**he is such a scuz. there's no way ANY girl would have sex with him.**
zoegirl:	so kurt said, "dude, ur crazy," as in, "ppl can hear, man," but chase was all, "chill, nobody's listening." kurt said, "what about her?" meaning me. chase laffed and said, "zoe? she doesn't even know what 'giving head' means." then he poked me in the back and goes, "do u, zoe? do u know what 'giving head' means?"
mad maddie:	**what a dick**
zoegirl:	so i turned around and looked him dead in the eye and said, "shut the hell up, chase."
zoegirl:	i really really did it!!!!!
mad maddie:	**whoa! nice work, zo!**
zoegirl:	i know
mad maddie:	**altho it's kinda pathetic that u c this as a big deal. any other girl would say that to him as a matter of course.**
zoegirl:	i took your dare, simple as that. don't go downplaying it now.
mad maddie:	**no, it's great. really.**
zoegirl:	doug said so 2. he was very proud of me.
mad maddie:	**uh huh. and how r things going with ol' dougie?**
zoegirl:	just fine, thanx very much. we went out for coffee after school, altho actually we had chai hot chocolates. have u ever tried them?

Send   Cancel

mad maddie:	**2 nutmeg-y for me. in a bad way.**
zoegirl:	i thought they were good. and doug and i had an awesome convo, which was even better.
zoegirl:	i *really* like him, maddie.
mad maddie:	**didn't u already *really* like him?**
zoegirl:	but now i like him even more. the physical stuff is still . . . a little rocky, but everything else is perfect. plus it's such a relief to like someone normal again, someone i'm allowed to like.
mad maddie:	**as opposed to mr. h?**
zoegirl:	as opposed to mr. h.
zoegirl:	i saw mr. h with cameron bryant today, btw. it kinda freaked me out. he was leaning close and smiling at her like he used to smile at me.
mad maddie:	**u know what i heard from some senior? that every year mr. h has a "special" female student that he pays a lot of attention to.**
mad maddie:	**i wasn't gonna tell u—but now i did.**
zoegirl:	oh
mad maddie:	**sick, huh?**
zoegirl:	yeah. sick.
mad maddie:	**so u should be doubly glad u've got doug, that's all i'm saying.**
zoegirl:	right, i am
mad maddie:	**and that doug isn't pervy like mr. h.**
mad maddie:	**or chase dickinson**
zoegirl:	u know what else chase said? that he used to have this girl he "hung" with who gave him head for over an hour. is that possible?

Send   Cancel

mad maddie:	**now that's just silly. blow jobs should not last over 30 minutes.**
zoegirl:	ewww!
mad maddie:	**ah, zoe, u still have a ways to go!**

Thursday, January 20, 4:04 PM P.S.T.

SnowAngel:	hey, zo. have u ever had Bingham Hill wasabi cheese spread? it is soooooo good.
zoegirl:	isn't wasabi that super spicy green stuff u get with sushi?
SnowAngel:	yeah, but this is a cheese spread with wasabi in it. it makes my mouth sting, but it's thoroughly addictive. *swipes last little bit up with cracker and smacks lips*
zoegirl:	mmm, ur making me hungry
zoegirl:	u wanna hear something sad? i saw mr. h hitting on cameron bryant—well, sitting really close to her in backwork—and maddie told me that she's his "special" student this year.
SnowAngel:	that's not sad. that's gross. he needs to go to a sex offenders' home.
zoegirl:	i know, i know
zoegirl:	but the reason it's sad is cuz when maddie told me that, it made *me* feel sad.
SnowAngel:	WHY?
zoegirl:	i dunno
zoegirl:	cuz i wanted to be the only one?
SnowAngel:	zoe, no. u r sooooooo much better off w/o him.

Send Cancel

163

SnowAngel:	i take it u and maddie r talking, tho, since she's the 1 who told u about him.
zoegirl:	sorta, i guess
zoegirl:	huh. wonder how that happened?
SnowAngel:	well that's terrif. see ya!

Saturday, January 22, 8:00 PM E.S.T.

mad maddie:	**can't talk long—meeting chive for a nite of wanton indulgence—but DUDE, am i brilliant. i have given zoe the best freakin dare ever.**
SnowAngel:	dare? what do u mean, dare?
mad maddie:	**it's just this thing we're doing. u gave me the idea, actually.**
SnowAngel:	i did?
mad maddie:	**i gave her the first 1 last week, and i just gave her the 2nd. it's freakin genius.**
SnowAngel:	what is it?
mad maddie:	**can't tell. top secret. but it's going down tomorrow, on sunday, the day of our lord.**
SnowAngel:	it's "going down"? what r u, a jewel thief?
mad maddie:	**please. we're not stealing anything—in fact, the opposite.**
mad maddie:	**heh heh heh, it's so perfect to do it while he's at church.**
SnowAngel:	do WHAT?
mad maddie:	**g2g. byeas!**
SnowAngel:	maddie! aargh!!!!!

Send Cancel

Saturday, January 22, 5:07 PM P.S.T.

SnowAngel: zoe, what r u and maddie up 2??? what's this "dare" business she's talking about?

Auto response from zoegirl: can't talk now—hanging out with the kiddos!

SnowAngel: hanging out with doug is more like it. admit it, the only reason u like your job is cuz of him.

SnowAngel: IM me!!!

Sunday, January 23, 11:23 AM E.S.T.

zoegirl: oh man, angela, r u up?

SnowAngel: yes, but only cuz U NEVER IMed ME LAST NITE and i'm dying to know what's going on!

zoegirl: omg, i haven't laffed like that in *forever*. at 1st i was like, "no, maddie, we can't!" but we did, and it was totally . . . purging.

SnowAngel: will u please explain what ur talking about?

zoegirl: we plastered bumper stickers all over mr. h's car while he was at church! we were very sneaky. we were like spies. and we stuck them on with super-glue so they'll be really really hard to get off!

SnowAngel: no way! what did they say?

zoegirl: 1 said "sticks and stones will break my bones, but whips and chains excite me," and another said "i'd rather be spanked."

zoegirl: also included were "ass pirate," "i heart llamas," and, my personal fave, "jesus loves you, but i'm his favorite."

Send   Cancel

165

SnowAngel:	holy cats. he's gonna die.
zoegirl:	he already did. maddie and i hid at the other end of the parking lot until church let out, and we watched him walk to his car. he was with some friends—including a woman!—and when he saw the bumper stickers, he about had a heart attack. the woman got a pissy look on her face, like she was all indignant on his behalf, but his other friends cracked up. it was *supremely* satisfying.
SnowAngel:	i'll bet
zoegirl:	it was also supremely satisfying to c him try to peel them off. hahaha.
SnowAngel:	right, hahaha
SnowAngel:	when did u guys decide to do this, anyway?
zoegirl:	we didn't really *decide* anything. maddie dared me to do it, and so i did.
SnowAngel:	how come u didn't tell me?
zoegirl:	oh. well . . . i guess it didn't occur to us.
SnowAngel:	it didn't OCCUR to u?
zoegirl:	it wasn't that big a deal.
zoegirl:	wait a sec, r u upset?
SnowAngel:	no, of course not. why would i be upset?
zoegirl:	if anything, i thought u'd be glad that maddie and i r doing stuff again.
SnowAngel:	i am, i am
zoegirl:	u want us to be happy, don't u?
SnowAngel:	i suppose
SnowAngel:	but maybe i don't want u to be DELIRIOUSLY happy, that's all.

Send   Cancel

zoegirl:	oh, angela
SnowAngel:	it IS pretty funny, tho. what u did.
zoegirl:	it would have been even better if u'd been with us—and i'm not just saying that!

Monday, January 24, 5:22 PM E.S.T.

mad maddie:	**hellooooo, zoe. prepare to face your darkest fears, for i am about to issue the best and most thrilling dare yet. r u ready?**
zoegirl:	what? no, i'm not ready.
mad maddie:	**well get ready, cuz this is not a dare to be denied. it is the Dare of the Century.**
zoegirl:	i hate to break it to u, but i think we should be done with dares.
mad maddie:	**done with dares? surely u josh!**
zoegirl:	i think we're making angela feel bad.
mad maddie:	**ohhhhh, the old "we're making angela feel bad" ploy. sorry, charlie, but i'm not letting u off the hook that easily.**
mad maddie:	**r u ready to hear the dare?**
zoegirl:	no
mad maddie:	**good, cuz first i need to give u some background information. imagine if u will a brightly lit classroom. it is 6th-period english, and all the students r filing in. but—what's this? instead of taking a seat, theresa ketchum scowls and drags her desk to the other side of the room. "theresa," mr. phelps says with a look of confusion, "why r u moving your desk?"**
zoegirl:	maddie, i'm serious—no more dares.

Send   Cancel

zoegirl:	plus, i just realized something: why r *u* the only 1 giving me dares? why don't i get to give *u* a dare?
mad maddie:	**and theresa says, "i'm moving my desk cuz i don't wanna stare at wendy's butt. her crack's worming out of her jeans."**
mad maddie:	**btw, didn't i point out long ago that low-riders r not for those who r substantially endowed in the buttock area? why yes, i believe i did.**
zoegirl:	i don't know where ur going with this, but i am not taking any more dares. and i am most definitely not taking any dares that have to do with butt cracks.
mad maddie:	**please, like i would show such poor taste. but watching this little slice of life got me thinking: what freaks zoe out more than anything? and my brain answered, "BODIES. bodies freak zoe out more than anything."**
zoegirl:	what? that is so not true!
mad maddie:	**so what does zoe need to do? zoe needs to loosen up. yes, that's right, she needs to overcome her fears of being a woman, with all that being a woman involves. she needs—drumroll, please—to embrace her sexuality!**
zoegirl:	no no no no no
mad maddie:	**the other dares have been warm-ups. rehearsals, if u will. for it is this ultimate dare that will bring u to the peak of self-awareness.**
zoegirl:	good grief, maddie. could u be a little less full of yourself?
mad maddie:	**here is your dare: u r to glue two marshmallows to your shirt—the OUTSIDE of your shirt—at approximate nipple location, then stroll from 1 end of the mall to the other.**

Send   Cancel

zoegirl:	*maddie*!
zoegirl:	u have lost it. i'm leaving now. bye-bye!
mad maddie:	**"the great marshmallow-nipple dare," i call it.**
mad maddie:	**is it illegal? nooooo. is it dangerous? nooooo. will ppl stare at u? hmm, they very well might. i would, if i saw some chick prancing along with marshmallows glued to her nipples.**
zoegirl:	there is no way i'm doing that, so just forget it!
mad maddie:	**then ur a wimp, and u finally have to admit it.**
zoegirl:	wait just a minute. i told chase dickinson to go to hell. i pasted lewd bumper stickers on mr. h's car. u can *not* tell me i'm a wimp!
mad maddie:	**but this one's the real dare, the dare that's about U. and if u don't take it, then u have to admit that ur afraid to live your life fully.**
zoegirl:	prancing around with marshmallows on your nipples does *not* constitute living your life fully!
mad maddie:	**wimp**
zoegirl:	this is so unfair! *no one* would do this dare!
mad maddie:	**i would, and u know it.**
mad maddie:	**it's very simple if u think about it. u just have to get over your inhibitions, which is something u've needed to do for a long time.**
zoegirl:	ur doing me a favor, is that what ur saying?
mad maddie:	**tell ya what, they can be mini-marshmallows.**
zoegirl:	gee, thanks
mad maddie:	**so?**
zoegirl:	noooooooooooooooo!

| Send | Cancel | | 169 |

mad maddie: all right, then. ur officially a wuss!

Monday, January 24, 5:36 PM E.S.T.

mad maddie: **P.S. i googlewhacked "marshmallow nipple." 24,000 hits!!!**

zoegirl: maddie, ur a freak

mad maddie: **i'm just saying, that's a lot of marshmallow nipples . . .**

zoegirl: once and for all, *no*!!!

Monday, January 24, 6:30 PM E.S.T.

zoegirl: angela! where have u been all afternoon? u told me to include u in things, but how can i if ur never there? i've been trying to reach u for over an hour—i really need to talk to u!

SnowAngel: i just this second got home from school, which, btw, sucked. time difference, remember?

SnowAngel: can i tell u something depressing?

zoegirl: uh, sure

SnowAngel: i was watching this girl during lunch, 1 of the many girls who have no idea i exist. she was sitting in the courtyard, talking to someone on her cell, and she was so animated. yip yip yip, like a little dog. and then she said good-bye and snapped shut her phone, and all of a sudden there was just . . . nothing. her face was blank, her body was blank, it was like she'd snapped herself shut along with her phone.

Send   Cancel

zoegirl:	yikes
SnowAngel:	and i thought, "that's me, that's totally me."
zoegirl:	i feel that way sometimes. like when i'm around other ppl, i put on this show of being interested and eager, and then when i'm alone, i don't always know who i am. and i think how if someone were watching, like my dead grandfather or God or someone, all they'd see is this incredibly boring person.
SnowAngel:	for me it's u guys who make me feel alive, u and maddie. without u, i'm just this floating blob of nothingness.
zoegirl:	angela, ur not a floating blob of nothingness
SnowAngel:	seriously, i am!
SnowAngel:	someone had on a shirt today that said, "if i seem to be getting smaller, it's because i'm walking away." that's me, zo. i'm getting smaller and smaller, only i don't WANNA be walking away.
zoegirl:	oh, angela
SnowAngel:	*recedes into smaller and smaller dot and then POOF! disappears*
zoegirl:	u r never never never gonna disappear
SnowAngel:	what do u think my aunt sadie would do if i just showed up on her doorstep? she couldn't turn me away, could she?
zoegirl:	um. . .
SnowAngel:	aaargh, i don't mean to be so boring *gives self firm shake*
SnowAngel:	so what'd u IM about? u said u needed to talk.
zoegirl:	oh, right

Send   Cancel

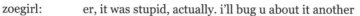

zoegirl:	er, it was stupid, actually. i'll bug u about it another time.
SnowAngel:	u sure? cuz if ur sure, i think i'm gonna go take a nap.
zoegirl:	well, try to feel better, ok?
SnowAngel:	ttfn!

Tuesday, January 25, 9:59 AM E.S.T.

mad maddie:	**u gonna do it?**
zoegirl:	leave me alone, i'm supposed to be doing research.
mad maddie:	**maybe we should ask peaches what she thinks. why look, there she is at her desk. should i call her over?**
zoegirl:	leave peaches out of it!
mad maddie:	**at least i didn't set the great marshmallow-nipple dare at school, zoe.**
mad maddie:	**think about it!!!**

Tuesday, January 25, 2:07 PM E.S.T.

mad maddie:	**u gonna do it?**
zoegirl:	*no*!

Tuesday, January 25, 9:41 PM E.S.T.

mad maddie:	**u gonna do it?**
zoegirl:	go away!!!!!!!!!!!!!!!!

Send   Cancel

Wednesday, January 26, 3:35 PM E.S.T.

mad maddie: ur not gonna do it, r u? i mean, not that i care. i'm just saying.

zoegirl: oh, right, u don't care. that's why u've been buzzing in my ear like a fly for the last 5,000 years. if i had a swatter, i'd swat u flat.

mad maddie: i only care cuz i care about U. i don't want u going thru life like a scared little mealworm, that's all. isn't it better to be a fly than a mealworm?

zoegirl: what?

mad maddie: quiet desperation . . . quiet desperation . . . quiet desperation . . .

zoegirl: fine, u freak. meet me at the mall in half an hour.

mad maddie: seriously?

zoegirl: but afterward, u belong to me. i'm gonna give u the worst possible dare ever so u'll know what it feels like!

mad maddie: wh-hoo! i'll bring the marshmallows!!!

Wednesday, January 26, 6:48 PM P.S.T.

SnowAngel: uh, maddie?

mad maddie: hey, angela! man, what a day. wazzup?

SnowAngel: i just got a really strange email from mary kate. she hasn't been in touch at all since i moved, and now she emails me this wacko message about zoe. u don't know anything about this, do u?

mad maddie: u got an email from mk? omg, this is great. what did she say?

SnowAngel:	she said she saw zoe at the mall and that zoe had MARSHMALLOWS GLUED TO HER NIPPLES! *bores eyes into friend in extreme concern*
mad maddie:	**it was awesome, angela. u should have been there.**
SnowAngel:	it's TRUE? oh my freakin god. cuz zoe won't answer my calls, and all i could think was, "maddie. maddie is behind this."
SnowAngel:	u made her glue marshmallows to her nipples?!!
mad maddie:	**well, to her shirt, not her actual bare skin. and i didn't MAKE her. it was a dare.**
SnowAngel:	another 1 of your stupid dares? that's sick!
mad maddie:	**don't think "sick," think . . . whimsical. playful. a breath of fresh air.**
SnowAngel:	i can't believe she actually did it. i can't believe it.
mad maddie:	**imagine if u will: the mall is packed with irritable shoppers, bored to tears with their predictable lives. but hark! from the distance comes a hazy apparition! it's . . . it's . . . it's zoe! she's charging thru the crowd, nipples a-blazin'!**
SnowAngel:	omg
mad maddie:	**her face was bright red and she kept her eyes straight ahead, playing the "if i can't c u, then u can't c me" game. she was walking so fast that ppl had to dive out of her way. if it wasn't for the security guard, she'd have been home free.**
SnowAngel:	the security guard?!!
mad maddie:	**but now zoe can add "run-in with the law" to her resume, 2. i'm so proud of her.**
SnowAngel:	but is she ok?? this is like her worst nightmare. she must be so completely thoroughly mortified!

Send   Cancel

mad maddie: if only she'd made it to Macy's. there was a group of nuns out front collecting money for the poor.

mad maddie: damn that pesky security guard!

SnowAngel: *shakes head in disbelief*

SnowAngel: u don't understand, maddie. zoe isn't equipped to handle something like this. if i was there, i would have stopped u!

mad maddie: but u weren't, were u? heh heh heh!

SnowAngel: i'm gonna try zoe again. she's probably buried herself in a hole and will never come out.

SnowAngel: u should be ashamed of yourself, madigan kinnick!

Wednesday, January 26, 7:20 PM P.S.T.

SnowAngel: still no answer. i'm really worried.

mad maddie: oh pshaw

SnowAngel: so does she get to dare U to do something, now that u've publicly humiliated her?

mad maddie: yeah, i have to do whatever she tells me to do. i'm sure she's gonna make me quit smoking pot, but i don't care. i was gonna quit anywayz.

SnowAngel: really?

SnowAngel: i mean, good! serves u right!

Thursday, January 27, 3:46 PM P.S.T.

SnowAngel: zoe, thank god. why haven't u answered your phone? r u 2 embarrassed to talk to anyone?

SnowAngel:	sweetie, u should have answered anyway—u don't have to be embarrassed in front of ME!
zoegirl:	huh?
zoegirl:	i guess my ringer's on mute. oops.
SnowAngel:	well i just want to say how SORRY i am that maddie did that to u. i don't know what she was thinking. and i'm so sorry u felt like u couldn't tell me, that day when u IMed and said u wanted to talk, only i was so depressed that all we did was talk about ME. i'm so sorry i let u down!
zoegirl:	angela, hold on. u didn't let me down, ok?
SnowAngel:	ur nice to say that, but i know i did.
SnowAngel:	i called u 5,000 times yesterday and never got u. what were u doing—hiding out under your covers?
zoegirl:	well actually . . .
zoegirl:	i *was* under the covers, but they weren't mine. and i wasn't exactly hiding . . .
SnowAngel:	i don't get it. what do u mean they weren't
SnowAngel:	OMG, what r u saying???
zoegirl:	oh man, angela. it was nuts. the security guard at the mall lectured me for half an hour about "proper behavior for young ladies"—while maddie stood there smirking!—and after that, i was so embarrassed that i fled to my car and zoomed off. i just wanted out of there, u know? but then about halfway home, i was filled with this incredible rush.
SnowAngel:	cuz it was over, u mean?
zoegirl:	no, cuz i *did* it!!! i actually did maddie's ridiculous

Send   Cancel

	dare. and having that knowledge inside me was like, WOW.
zoegirl:	it made me feel so liberated!
SnowAngel:	yes, but the covers . . .
SnowAngel:	just how liberated were u?
zoegirl:	liberated enuff to drive straight to doug's house instead of going home. his mom wasn't there, and we had the whole house to ourselves. and it was really, really great.
SnowAngel:	*gulps* r u saying what i think ur saying?
zoegirl:	no, angela, we didn't have sex. geez.
zoegirl:	but we went further than we've ever gone before, and the best part is, i just let myself enjoy it. i was, like, on this adrenaline high, and i felt like i could do anything. so i just let go of all my zoe stupidnesses and went for it.
SnowAngel:	oh
SnowAngel:	here i was imagining u in the depths of depression, and i felt so bad that i wasn't there for u, while all the time . . .
SnowAngel:	u really DIDN'T need me, huh?
zoegirl:	oh, angela. i *always* need u. don't u know that?
SnowAngel:	i can't believe things worked out so well for u. i mean . . . whoa.
zoegirl:	it *was* whoa. i never knew my body could feel like that. i know that sounds retarded.
SnowAngel:	it doesn't sound retarded. it sounds . . . u know. like a good thing.
zoegirl:	i've always felt so out of it when it comes to that stuff. like how i told u i could never get out of my brain, remember?

SnowAngel:	i remember. u wanted to be less inhibited.
zoegirl:	yeah, like maddie. i've never admitted this to anyone, but i've always been kinda jealous of her, of how easy it is for her to give herself over to the moment. secretly, i've always wished i was like that.
zoegirl:	not in a fool-around-with-every-guy-that-shows-up kind of way, but i didn't wanna be frigid, either. isn't that an awful word? i hate that word.
SnowAngel:	what, frigid? it doesn't sound like u need to worry about it anymore.
zoegirl:	that's what makes me so happy! cuz i *did* let go of my inhibitions and i *did* lose myself in the moment! and not to get 2 graphic or anything, but i was like, "damn, so *this* is what all the fuss is about!"
zoegirl:	i think doug enjoyed it, 2
SnowAngel:	nooooo, u think?
zoegirl:	all day long i've felt so strong inside, even when mary kate announced to our whole math class about the marshmallow-nipple thing. i just laffed like, "yeah? so?" and everyone looked at me like they couldn't believe it. like, "this is not the zoe we know."
SnowAngel:	r u saying ur GLAD maddie made that dare?
zoegirl:	no, i'm just saying . . . i dunno. that maybe it's not so bad to say "screw it" to the rules sometimes.
SnowAngel:	oh *blinks in amazement*
zoegirl:	wanna hear something awful, tho? in my mad panic from the mall, i completely forgot about the marshmallows. so when i showed up at doug's, they were still there!

Send   Cancel

SnowAngel:	oh no! what did he do?
zoegirl:	let's just say that once i explained the whole crazy story, he took care of the problem. as in, the marshmallows r no more.
SnowAngel:	uh huh. what a gentleman.
zoegirl:	yeah, i love him
SnowAngel:	for real? u "love" him love him?
zoegirl:	omg, i didn't mean to say that. it just slipped out.
zoegirl:	but . . . shit, angela. i think i do.
SnowAngel:	*whistles* this is big
zoegirl:	it *feels* big
zoegirl:	hey, thanks for listening, angela. i'm sure it's boring to hear me go on and on.
SnowAngel:	um, no. boring is sitting alone in my room while everyone in my life moves on without me.
SnowAngel:	i'm happy for u, zoe, i truly am, but i swear i'm turning invisible.
zoegirl:	invisible? what do u mean?
SnowAngel:	last nite at dinner i didn't say a single word. i didn't have anything to say, so i just sat there and ate my peas. no one even noticed.
zoegirl:	i'm sure they noticed. that's so unlike u not to be chattering away.
SnowAngel:	nope, cuz later i brought it up to my mom, and she was like, "oh, angie, u did so talk. of course u did."
zoegirl:	hmm. not the most reassuring response.
SnowAngel:	everybody else's lives r so exciting that they forget i even exist.

zoegirl:	oh crap, angela, i am so sorry, but i've g2g. the doorbell just rang downstairs, and it's doug.
SnowAngel:	oh
zoegirl:	i'll call u soon, i promise!!!

Friday, January 28, 10:03 AM E.S.T.

mad maddie:	**ah, we meet again in the lovely media center. so give me my stupid dare already, will ya? enuff with the taunting looks, just get on with it.**
zoegirl:	do u ever actually do your work when ur here? ever?
mad maddie:	**i already know what it's gonna be, so don't think ur gonna pull 1 over on me.**
zoegirl:	u know what it is, do u? then why don't u tell me?
mad maddie:	**go on, just say it**
zoegirl:	u want your dare? fine, here's your dare: tell chive how u really feel about him.
mad maddie:	**WHAT? that's not the dare ur supposed to give me!**
mad maddie:	**no way, try again**
zoegirl:	that's the dare. r u a mealworm, or r u a fly?
mad maddie:	**that's a stupid dare. that's the most stupid dare u could have possibly come up with.**
zoegirl:	oh yeah? then why is your face all red? i can c u, u know.
zoegirl:	hey, maybe we should ask peaches what she thinks. why look, there she is at her desk. shall i call her over?
mad maddie:	**chive doesn't like me. he likes whitney.**
zoegirl:	then why does he kiss u? and why do u let him? and why

Send   Cancel

| | r u packing up your books all of a sudden? has it gotten 2 hot in here for u? |
| zoegirl: | tell him how u feel. that's your dare!!! |

Saturday, January 29, 11:33 PM E.S.T.

zoegirl:	hey, angela, i can't believe ur up so late. isn't it like two in the morning there?
SnowAngel:	good god, zoe, i'm gonna have to strap a time-change clock to your forehead.
SnowAngel:	if it's 11:30 there, then it's 8:30 here, which means UR the one who's up late, at least for u. were u out with doug?
zoegirl:	yeah, we went out after work. but i'm not IMing about doug for once. i'm IMing to tell u what graham cracker said.
SnowAngel:	that 3-yr-old u think is so adorable?
zoegirl:	he fell and skinned his knee, and he got all worried when he saw that he was bleeding. it was just the tiniest bit, but he clamped his hand over the bloody spot and said, "i am holding it in. i am holding it in." like if he didn't, it might all drain out.
SnowAngel:	poor little guy
zoegirl:	finally he let me put a band-aid on. he watched me really carefully, and then his eyes welled up and he said, "zoe, i miss my mommy." and i said, "i know. she'll be here soon." and he said, "i miss her cuz i love her. and when i love ppl, i want them with me always."
SnowAngel:	awww

Send   Cancel

zoegirl:	and it made my heart hurt, and i thought of u.
zoegirl:	that's all.

Monday, January 31, 4:02 PM E.S.T.

mad maddie:	hey, zo. i'm at java joe's right now—and guess who i ran into in line?
zoegirl:	who?
mad maddie:	ian! with margo pedersen! THEY WERE HOLDING HANDS!
zoegirl:	ooo, maddie, ouch.
zoegirl:	u ok?
mad maddie:	am i ok? hell yeah i'm ok. it was a classic awkward moment, tho, the ex meeting the new flame. ian was like, "uh, maddie, this is, um, margo. she's, um . . . well, we were just . . . " and i was like, "dude, i know who margo is. we go to the same school. and ur allowed to date someone new, u know."
zoegirl:	weren't u the teeniest bit upset?
mad maddie:	i did have the uncharitable thought of "she has a big ass, ha ha ha." but oddly enuff i wasn't that upset. wanna know why?
zoegirl:	why?
mad maddie:	cuz i don't like ian anymore. i mean, as a human being, sure. but i'm not pining over him in the slightest.
zoegirl:	ahhh
mad maddie:	he's not chive, that's the basic point.
zoegirl:	so ur admitting loud and clear in the light of day that U LIKE CHIVE. that's good, maddie. that's very good. now u just have to tell *him*.

Send   Cancel

mad maddie:	**wait for it, wait for it**
mad maddie:	**i'm gonna tell him this weekend. we're gonna hang on saturday—i'll tell him then.**
zoegirl:	for real?!
mad maddie:	**i haven't done it YET. but i figure If u can glue marshmallows to your nipples . . .**
zoegirl:	doug calls me "hot cocoa" now, btw. warm and luscious with a delightful marshmallow topping.
mad maddie:	**good god, 1 little dare and out comes your inner deviant.**
zoegirl:	ha ha ha. doug said the same thing, actually . . .
mad maddie:	**he should send me flowers. he owes me BIG time.**
mad maddie:	**i'm outta here—i finished my chai and i've got some errands to run.**
zoegirl:	oh yeah? whatcha doing?
mad maddie:	**never u mind. it has to do with angela (and MAYBE u if ur nice), and it's a surprise. i just hate it that she's so depressed. it kills me.**
zoegirl:	i know
zoegirl:	but she left a message on my voicemail saying her mom's driving her into the city this afternoon, so that should help.
mad maddie:	**that reminds me, the other thing i need to do is swing by the DMV and apply for a new driver's license. every time i drive somewhere, i think, "shit, what if i get pulled over."**
zoegirl:	why do u need a new license?
mad maddie:	**cuz i lost mine, didn't i tell u? byeas!**

Send   Cancel   183

Monday, January 31, 8:24 PM P.S.T.

SnowAngel: maddie, my life has hit an all-time low.

mad maddie: oh no. what happened?

SnowAngel: i know that hardly seems possible. how could i be lower than i already was? yet here i am.

mad maddie: i thought u went into the city today. i thought u loved the city!

SnowAngel: i do love the city—it's the only good thing about being here. but guess who i saw while i was there? actually don't bother, cuz u never will. i was buying a hot dog at the embarcadero, and the girl in front of me looked vaguely familiar. she turned around and it was JEANNIE STARR.

mad maddie: jeannie starr? she goes to northside, doesn't she? i think she's one grade above chive.

SnowAngel: yeah, she's a senior. that's why she was in san francisco, cuz she was visiting colleges. she says she wants to get as far away from home as possible.

SnowAngel: isn't that ironic? i was like, "here, u can have my life. wanna trade?"

mad maddie: that is so weird that u ran into her. i don't know that i'd even recognize her.

SnowAngel: it took us both a minute, cuz i barely know her and she barely knows me. but then she said, "wait a sec . . . aren't u angela silver? i thought u were dead!"

mad maddie: DEAD?

SnowAngel: she said, "i thought u died in a car wreck! that's what someone told me!"

Send   Cancel

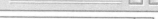

SnowAngel:	this is what my life has come to, maddie. i move away, and 1 month later everyone assumes i'm dead!
mad maddie:	**that is so sad**
SnowAngel:	i said to jeannie, "what? no, i'm not dead." and she goes, "r u sure?"
mad maddie:	**good grief. she is 1 donut short of a dozen.**
SnowAngel:	i stuck out my arm and said, "u can pinch me if u want." and she did!!!
mad maddie:	**man. it's like that mark twain quote, "the reports of my death have been greatly exaggerated."**
SnowAngel:	but the reports of my pathetic-ness have not. i might as well be dead.
mad maddie:	**DON'T EVEN SAY THAT. EVER!!!**
SnowAngel:	and then—THEN—i came home to find glendy's name on our caller ID 13 times. what could anybody have to say that's that important?
mad maddie:	**how do u know it was the glendinizer? maybe it was mr. boss, calling for your dad.**
SnowAngel:	nuh uh, cuz she didn't leave a message, which mr. boss would have done. anyway, dad was at work, so mr. boss would have seen him there.
mad maddie:	**did u call her back?**
SnowAngel:	no, i hit delete, delete, delete. *jabs button 13 times*
mad maddie:	**lord, angela**
SnowAngel:	and now i am going to go take a very long, very hot bath and use up all of my mom's aromatherapy beads, and even that will not wash away the stain of my pathetic-ness.

Send Cancel

185

SnowAngel: i love u, maddie, but i hate my life!!!

Monday, January 31, 9:15 PM P.S.T.

SnowAngel: glendy called AGAIN. can i tell u what was so desperately important?

mad maddie: sure

SnowAngel: apparently she felt unloved. apparently she'd saved me a seat at lunch today and i failed to notice.

mad maddie: so?

SnowAngel: well, yeah, exactly! i was like, "and this was so important that u had to call me 13 frickin times???"

mad maddie: technically, 14

SnowAngel: all i could think was, "great. everyone thinks i'm DEAD except for u, and ur the 1 person in the world i don't wanna hang out with. LEAVE ME ALONE, U FREAK!"

mad maddie: ha

mad maddie: what'd u tell her for real?

SnowAngel: seriously, maddie, i couldn't take it anymore, so i was kinda mean. i said, "i'm sorry i didn't c u flagging me down. clearly i am a worthless human being. next time just don't bother, ok?"

mad maddie: ooo, way to tell it like it is

mad m1addie: what did SHE say?

SnowAngel: 1st there was dead silence, and then she said really coldly, "well, excuse me for trying to be nice. excuse me for thinking u actually wanted a friend. u pretend to be so sweet, but really ur just a bitch!"

Send   Cancel

mad maddie:	**omg**
mad maddie:	**angela, that was so un-called for. SHE'S the bitch—u know that, right?**
SnowAngel:	it made me cry, maddie, isn't that ridiculous? after she hung up on me, i just sat on my bed and bawled.
mad maddie:	**oh, sweetie**
mad maddie:	**if i were there, i'd spray paint bad words on her locker for u. i'd take away all her Care Bears!**
SnowAngel:	*sniffles pathetically*
mad maddie:	**just think of it this way: maybe u've gotten rid of the glendinizer once and for all.**
SnowAngel:	god, let's hope
SnowAngel:	i'm going to call zoe and tell her about this stupidness, and then i'm going to bed.
SnowAngel:	thanks for listening, mads. nite!!!

Tuesday, February 1, 6:33 PM E.S.T.

zoegirl:	angela—finally! i *hate* this 3 hour time difference. i've been waiting forever for u to get home from school!
SnowAngel:	yeah? wassup?
zoegirl:	i wanna ask your advice about something—but 1st u have to update me on the glendy situation. how was she when u saw her today???
SnowAngel:	*makes guttural frankenstein noise*
zoegirl:	not so good, huh?
SnowAngel:	actually it was fine, in that she totally ignored me. u

Send   Cancel   187

	know the drill: wounded cold shoulder and poisonous glares. but at least i have her off my back, right?
zoegirl:	*absolutely*
zoegirl:	i'm still sorry that happened, tho
SnowAngel:	oh who cares. it's just like everything else in my life, a big pile of poo.
SnowAngel:	so what's going on with u? what do u need my advice on?
zoegirl:	well . . . my mom and dad r going to this big law firm shindig on saturday nite. it's called the prom, isn't that dorky?
SnowAngel:	your mom and dad r going to the prom?
zoegirl:	it's really just a fancy party, with a seated dinner and a live band. but it's black tie, so everyone gets all dressed up. 1 of the partners decided to call it the prom as a joke.
SnowAngel:	oh those crazy grown-ups
zoegirl:	but what this means is that i will have the house to myself.
zoegirl:	eeek! i'm so excited!
SnowAngel:	aha. r u gonna invite doug over?
zoegirl:	i wanna cook him a really nice dinner, wouldn't that be fun? and then . . . who knows where the evening will lead?
SnowAngel:	hold on now. ur not thinking . . . i mean, ur not planning to . . .
zoegirl:	no! u always ask that, and the answer is always no. the answer will *always* be no, ok?
zoegirl:	but there's a lot u can do leading up to that . . .
SnowAngel:	an empty house, a romantic dinner, a soft, inviting bed . . .

Send   Cancel

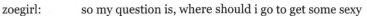

zoegirl:	so my question is, where should i go to get some sexy lingerie?
SnowAngel:	zoe! *jaw drops on floor*
zoegirl:	what? that's allowed, isn't it?
SnowAngel:	of course it's allowed! i'm just flabbergasted. who'd have thought that u, of all ppl, would be marching off to buy sexy lingerie? and for doug!!!
zoegirl:	where should i go? victoria's secret?
SnowAngel:	sure, that would work. what r u gonna get?
zoegirl:	that's what u need to tell me. what *should* i get?
SnowAngel:	hmmm *taps finger on chin*
SnowAngel:	is this something u plan to model for him, or will it just be the delightful surprise beneath your clothes?
zoegirl:	i'm not gonna model it for him! no, no, no. just something nice for when we . . . u know.
SnowAngel:	then i'd say it's time to go for the thong, zoe. god knows ur the only girl on the planet who doesn't own one.
zoegirl:	a thong? that sounds so scary.
zoegirl:	anyway, don't u have to have a really good butt to wear a thong?
SnowAngel:	u DO have a really good butt. look, here's the criteria for a thong: firm butt (preferably tan), no dimples, no unruly hairs. do u meet the requirements?
zoegirl:	ew, angela. does anyone really have hair on her butt?
SnowAngel:	well, not sprouting from the cheeks or anything. i'm talking about from within the crevice.
zoegirl:	angela! sick!

Send   Cancel

SnowAngel:	so, good. u don't have butt hair—u can cross that off the list. now, for the firmness element. *cups hands in air as if squeezing* i don't think u have any problem there.
zoegirl:	oh my god, i am getting so nervous just talking about this.
zoegirl:	but ok, a thong. *maybe*. what about on top?
SnowAngel:	just get a good push-up bra with a little lace or ribbon on it. u'll be able to find one to match the thong.
zoegirl:	i will?
SnowAngel:	if u can't, just ask one of the sales ladies to help u.
zoegirl:	no way, 2 embarrassing
zoegirl:	aye-yai-yai—i wish u were here to go with me!
SnowAngel:	yeah, me 2 *crumples into sad sack of a person*
zoegirl:	oh no, have i made u sad?
SnowAngel:	no sadder than i already was.
SnowAngel:	i'll be with u in spirit, all right? now go shop, u love-crazed fool!

Tuesday, February 1, 8:11 PM P.S.T.

SnowAngel:	hi, maddie. i am feeling very worthless. wanna know why?
mad maddie:	**why?**
SnowAngel:	cuz zoe IMed earlier to ask for fashion advice, and it made me so aware of how pointless my life has become. she has doug, u have chive—and more than that, u both have each other. but what do i have? a

Send   Cancel

	big fat nothing. i don't even have glendy now that she's stopped talking to me!
mad maddie:	**but that's a good thing, remember?**
mad maddie:	**anyway, i don't "have" chive. not even close.**
SnowAngel:	except ur gonna confess your love to him on saturday, zoe told me. and then he's gonna throw himself in your arms and ur gonna waltz off in a spasm of happiness.
SnowAngel:	i, probably, will be at home staring at my toenails.
mad maddie:	**that's bullshit**
mad maddie:	**do u really think he's gonna throw himself in my arms?**
SnowAngel:	so to commemorate my sadness, i've shaved off all my hair. i just wanted to let u know.
mad maddie:	**WHAT? u've been trying so long to grow it out!**
SnowAngel:	yeah, but what's the point? i don't have anyone to look good for, so i shaved it all off. i can be daring 2, u know.
mad maddie:	**wait a minute, no u can't. i see thru u like saran wrap, angela silver.**
SnowAngel:	well, i could have shaved it all off. i THOUGHT about it.
mad maddie:	**your hair is so pretty—don't shave it off.**
SnowAngel:	i'm just so depressed. i have to do something.
SnowAngel:	my mom says i can go to atlanta over spring break, but that's not good enuff. that's so far away!
mad maddie:	**ur coming to atlanta over spring break? angela, that's awesome!**
SnowAngel:	no it's not. i wanna be there now!
mad maddie:	**when's your spring break?**

Send   Cancel

SnowAngel:	march 21-25
mad maddie:	**that seems like a long way off, but c'mon. this is very very very good news.**
SnowAngel:	then why doesn't it feel like it? ☹
mad maddie:	**hold on, girl—u'll be here before u know it!**

Wednesday, February 2, 4:44 PM P.S.T.

SnowAngel:	well, i've started cutting myself. just fyi.
mad maddie:	**yeah, right. u can't stand the sound of your pulse, but i'm supposed to believe u could slice your skin and watch your blood ooze out?**
SnowAngel:	ugh ☺
SnowAngel:	u should go into counseling, maddie
mad maddie:	**what? i'm not the one with the problem here!**
SnowAngel:	i don't mean as a patient. i mean as a counselor. i can just see u talking to some poor distraught girl—much like ME, i might add—and saying, "u cut yourself, do u? u slice your skin and watch the blood ooze out?" u'd cure her in no time.
mad maddie:	**good. does that mean i cured u?**
SnowAngel:	maybe i'll start slow and build up. this girl in my math class uses a pink eraser to rub raw spots on the inside of her arm. i could manage that, i bet.
mad maddie:	**please don't hurt yourself, angela. even in jest.**
SnowAngel:	did zoe ever make it to victoria's secret?
mad maddie:	**ooo, baby. she just popped by to show me her purchases, and they're sexcellent.**

Send   Cancel

mad maddie: she didn't actually try them on for me, for which i say a prayer of thanks, but they look perfect. the bra is this filmy thing with lace and a little rosebud in the center, and she did, in fact, get a thong. i am extremely impressed.

SnowAngel: what's it look like, the thong?

mad maddie: er, like a thong. it's got the same little rosebud thing going on as the bra.

mad maddie: pelt-woman calls her jesus sandals "thongs," btw. i've tried and tried to correct her, but to no avail.

SnowAngel: can u imagine pelt-woman wearing a thong? a real thong?

mad maddie: i will now slide a steel door over my eyes to prevent that image from entering my brain. there r few things i could think of that would be more horrifying.

SnowAngel: my mom says that the key to a successful marriage is wearing pretty underwear. u might let pelt-woman know.

mad maddie: yeah, i'll get right on that.

mad maddie: your mom is something else, a.

SnowAngel: if u think she's bad, u should try my aunt sadie. i called her last nite and said, "please can't i come live with u? please please please please please?" and she was like, "angie, i would love nothing more than for u to come live with me. we'd be 2 hip girls on our own. but hon, that's between u and your parents."

SnowAngel: then she told me she had to go cuz she was getting ready for a date, but before she hung up, she gave me a handy tip which i should probably pass on to zoe.

Send   Cancel

mad maddie:	**which was?**
SnowAngel:	to lean over when ur putting your bra on and really jiggle your boobs into place. "so many women have an extra inch of cleavage that remains under-utilized," she told me. "it's over by your armpits. u just have to shove it into place."
mad maddie:	**armpit cleavage. luverly!**

Wednesday, February 2, 5:21 PM P.S.T.

SnowAngel:	hi, mads
mad maddie:	**u again? couldn't get enuff of me, is that it?**
SnowAngel:	i just wanted u to know how wrong u r about me, that's all. i may not be able to stand the sound of my pulse, but i'm quite fine with needles as it turns out.
mad maddie:	**so ur saying . . . what? u've taken up cross-stitch?**
SnowAngel:	i'm saying that i've pierced my nose. AND my nipple. i did it myself in my very own bathroom, just this second. *proudly thrusts out boob*
mad maddie:	**angela, cupcake, ur picking the entirely wrong audience for your charade. u need to be telling this to zoe, not me.**
mad maddie:	**anywayz, if ur going for shock value, u should tell her u pierced your labia.**
SnowAngel:	*eyes widen with appreciation* u r so right.
mad maddie:	**but don't say u did it yourself. that's 2 much of a stretch, even for zo.**
SnowAngel:	ah yes, good tip!

194

Wednesday, February 2, 5:30 PM P.S.T.

SnowAngel:	hi, zoe. i have something shocking to tell u, and i don't want u to get upset, ok?
zoegirl:	what happened? is something wrong?
SnowAngel:	no, no, nothing's wrong . . . other than everything, that is.
SnowAngel:	it's just, well . . .
SnowAngel:	i pierced my labia.
zoegirl:	*what*?
SnowAngel:	i pierced my labia. i got this sudden urge, i don't even know why, so i walked into a body-art salon and just went for it.
zoegirl:	omg. *oh my god*. did it hurt?
SnowAngel:	a little, yeah. well ok, a lot. but i was very brave. in fact, the guy who did the piercing said i was the bravest of anyone he'd done.
zoegirl:	a *guy* did it? why, angela???
SnowAngel:	cuz he was the only person there. he does tattoos, 2. do u think i should get a tattoo?
zoegirl:	angela, i don't know how to say this, but—and please don't be offended—is this a cry for help? sometimes ppl do really out-of-character things when they're unhappy. i mean, tattoos r fine, but do u honestly want to get one? u know how u r with needles.
SnowAngel:	oh, zoe. ur no fun.
SnowAngel:	no, i don't want a tattoo. and i don't want a pierced labia, either.

zoegirl:	so u *were* just doing it for attention! poor angela!
zoegirl:	just take out the ring or stud or whatever it is, and i bet the hole will grow over. u've only had it for a day, right?
SnowAngel:	even less. i never got it done, zo.
zoegirl:	what do u mean, u never got it done? u just said
zoegirl:	oh. haha.
SnowAngel:	sorry
zoegirl:	did maddie put u up to this???
SnowAngel:	*blinks meekly*
zoegirl:	i should have known. what was i thinking? u can't even stand the sound of your own pulse.
SnowAngel:	must everyone go on and on about that? YES, i'm a wimp. i admit it. u and maddie do these daring, exciting things, and what do i do? i plod thru school with glendy trailing behind me like a cloud of doom. even when i go to the bathroom, there she is, glaring malevolently at me from over the top of the stall.
zoegirl:	she does not stare at u from over the top of the stall.
zoegirl:	does she?
zoegirl:	anyway, what have i ever done that's so daring and exciting?
SnowAngel:	hmm, does parading thru the mall with marshmallow-nipples count? plus ur planning this fabulous nite with doug, which requires its own kind of daring. and while ur macking it up with him, maddie's gonna be confessing her undying love to chive. that's braver than all the stupid-ass stunts she's pulled before.
zoegirl:	well . . . ok, that's actually true. but ur brave 2, angela.

196

SnowAngel:	no, i'm not. if i was brave, i'd escape this stinking hell-hole!
zoegirl:	listen, angela. being in california isn't your fault, and being stalked by glendy isn't your fault either. just keep telling yourself, "spring break. spring break, spring break, spring break."
SnowAngel:	u think it's that easy, but it's not. i can't talk about it anymore—it's only making things worse. i'm signing off.
zoegirl:	i don't think it's easy. i just don't c any alternative.
zoegirl:	angela?
zoegirl:	just remember we love u, no matter how far away u r!!!

Thursday, February 3, 6:02 PM E.S.T.

zoegirl:	hey, mads. can't talk long—i'm heading out to dinner with my parents. i figure i should play the good girl role while i can so that they won't suspect anything about saturday nite.
mad maddie:	**have u worked out the details with doug?**
zoegirl:	my mom and dad leave for the prom at 7, so i'll start cooking then. i'm making chicken parmesan, steamed broccoli, and crescent rolls. doesn't that sound good?
mad maddie:	**i thought for a romantic evening u were supposed to eat oysters.**
zoegirl:	yeah, like i know how to cook oysters. if i even liked oysters, which i don't. anyway, i told doug to show up at 8. i don't want him coming over until the food is in the oven.

mad maddie:	**what about kidding around? don't u guys usually work on saturday nites?**
zoegirl:	we traded shirts.
mad maddie:	**u traded SHIRTS?**
zoegirl:	oops, i meant *shifts*. this is our 1 opportunity to have the house to ourselves. i intend to take advantage of every minute of it.
mad maddie:	**yeah, so that u can trade shirts, heh heh heh.**
zoegirl:	that was pretty freudian, huh?
zoegirl:	i'm *nervous*, maddie. isn't that silly?
mad maddie:	**it's cuz ur having impure thoughts. just think, after saturday u'll be a soiled dove.**
zoegirl:	a soiled . . . ?
zoegirl:	maddie, no. i told u already—we're not gonna have sex.
mad maddie:	**says who?**
zoegirl:	says me! *and* doug. we're not ready.
mad maddie:	**u say ur not ready, but what happens when the passion of the moment overtakes u? do u have a condom just in case?**
zoegirl:	oh, and where am i supposed to get a condom? u think i'm just gonna march into the drugstore and
zoegirl:	*stop*! i am not having this convo! doug and i r gonna have a lovely romantic evening together, and maybe we'll fool around and maybe we won't.
mad maddie:	**believe me, u will**
zoegirl:	but either way, we're *not* gonna have sex.
zoegirl:	now enuff about me. what about u? have u planned what ur gonna say to chive?

mad maddie:	**ur joking, right?**
zoegirl:	if ur gonna confess your love to him, u need to know what ur gonna say. these things require thought.
mad maddie:	**cuz ur the expert now?**
mad maddie:	**listen, zo. i'm not a plan-it-out kind of girl.**
zoegirl:	have u thought about it at all?
mad maddie:	**dude, i have sweat stains the size of buffaloes blooming from under my pits.**
zoegirl:	ick, maddie!
mad maddie:	**just imagine how bad i'll be by saturday when i actually c him. THIS is why i don't wanna think about it. i'll just . . . say whatever i happen to say. don't stress me out, ok?**
zoegirl:	fine, just as long as u don't wimp out. just remember: marshmallows!!!
mad maddie:	**grrrr**
zoegirl:	ack, my mom's yelling that it's time to go.
zoegirl:	real quick, have u heard from angela today?
mad maddie:	**no, have u?**
zoegirl:	she called from her cell a few hours ago, while she was still at school. it was a little strange.
mad maddie:	**strange how?**
zoegirl:	cuz 3 minutes into our conversation, she said, "oh, crap. here comes glendy."
mad maddie:	**i thought glendy was giving her the cold shoulder.**
zoegirl:	that's exactly what i said. and angela said, "i thought so 2, but she's heading straight for me. and she's wearing a VEST."
mad maddie:	**i don't get it. what's the significance of a vest?**

Send   Cancel

zoegirl:	i dunno, that they're tacky?
zoegirl:	then in the background i heard this whiny voice, which i assume was glendy, saying, "angela? can we talk?"
zoegirl:	and then angela told me she had to go, but that she'd call me right back. and then she hung up.
mad maddie:	**huh. i wonder what happened.**
zoegirl:	and *i* wonder why she hasn't called me back.
zoegirl:	all right, g2g for real. bye!

Thursday, February 3, 9:33 PM E.S.T.

zoegirl:	where in the world is angela? i just got home from dinner, and there wasn't a single message!!
mad maddie:	**give it a rest. she's FINE.**
zoegirl:	u don't think she's gone off and done something crazy, do u?
mad maddie:	**ANGELA? no, i don't think she's gone off and done something crazy.**
mad maddie:	**unless maybe it involves a daringly sparkly eyeshadow . . .**
zoegirl:	all right, all right. i'm going to bed!

Friday, February 4, 6:59 PM E.S.T.

zoegirl:	maddie, this is serious. angela's cell is turned off, and she hasn't been on-line for 2 days. i called her land line, and her mom says she's at *glendy's*!
mad maddie:	**at glendy's?**

Send   Cancel

mad maddie:	**huh, that's unexpected**
zoegirl:	"unexpected"? that's all u can say?
mad maddie:	**what do u want me to say?**
zoegirl:	i want u to say that there's something very wrong with this picture, more than just "unexpected."
zoegirl:	she's disappeared off the face of the earth, and we're supposed to believe she's at *glendy's*?
mad maddie:	**she hasn't disappeared off the face of the earth. sheesh. sure, her cell's turned off, but she probably just spaced it. as for not being on-line, she just hasn't been on-line when U'VE been on-line. did u think of that?**
mad maddie:	**unless . . .**
zoegirl:	unless what?
mad maddie:	**unless the glendinizer locked angela into the basement and forced her into a vest!!! ahhhhhhhhhhhh!**
zoegirl:	shut up
mad maddie:	**maybe she and glendy had to do a school project or something. look up glendy's number and call her there.**
zoegirl:	do u know her last name?
mad maddie:	**sorry, charlie, ur on your own. l8rs!**

Friday, February 4, 11:59 PM M.S.T.

SnowAngel: hi, zo. it's super duper late, i know.

Auto response from zoegirl: We cannot cure the world of sorrows, but we can choose to live in joy.

SnowAngel: ooo, nice quote. who's it by?

SnowAngel: la la la, i wish u were awake.

Send	Cancel	
		201

SnowAngel: wake up, zoe! wake up!

SnowAngel: can u tell i don't know what to do with myself at midnight with no one to talk to?

SnowAngel: ok, well, i'll call u if i need u. bye!

Saturday, February 5, 12:04 AM M.S.T.

SnowAngel: maddie, ur not asleep 2, r u?

Auto response from mad maddie: honk shoooooo, honk shoooooo

SnowAngel: what's that supposed to be, u snoring?

SnowAngel: *drums fingers on scratchy upholstery*

SnowAngel: fine. just don't call me unpredictable ever again!!!

Saturday, February 5, 11:00 AM E.S.T.

zoegirl: maddie! i finally heard from angela, but it was a weird late-night phone IM.

mad maddie: **yeah? she IMed me, 2. she made a cryptic comment about not being unpredictable, i guess cuz for once she was up past me.**

mad maddie: **oh, and something about upholstery which i didn't get.**

zoegirl: well, i feel better knowing that at least she still exists. altho her phone is once more turned off, the rat.

mad maddie: **dude, it's 8 in the morning california time. of course her phone's turned off.**

zoegirl: oh. right.

mad maddie: **matter of fact, i'm going back to bed myself. gotta rest up for my evening of sin and debauchery.**

202

Send   Cancel

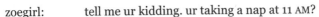

zoegirl:	tell me ur kidding. ur taking a nap at 11 AM?
mad maddie:	**nitey-nites!**

Saturday, February 5, 7:29 PM E.S.T.

zoegirl:	excuse me, but what r u doing still at home? why aren't u at chive's?
mad maddie:	**we're not meeting until after northside's basketball game, cuz whitney insisted they attend.**
mad maddie:	**why aren't u cooking your fancy dinner?**
zoegirl:	i already have. everything's in the oven, and all i've got left to do is decide what to wear. what do u think: jeans and my peasant blouse or my black j. crew skirt and my gray cashmere sweater?
mad maddie:	**i thought u were gonna wear your fancy underwear.**
zoegirl:	but what about on top? i'm not gonna open the door in my bra and thong, maddie.
mad maddie:	**well don't ask me. ask angela.**
zoegirl:	don't u think i would have if i'd ever been able to reach her???
mad maddie:	**ooo, touchy-touchy**
zoegirl:	so what should i wear??? doug's gonna be here in 20 minutes!
mad maddie:	**hmm. your peasant blouse is one of those off-the-shoulder dealies, right? i say wear that, for easy access.**
zoegirl:	easy access to what?
zoegirl:	never mind. god, maddie, u and your smutty mind. i'm wearing the sweater.

Send   Cancel

mad maddie:	u ask for my fashion advice and then do the exact opposite? what kind of friend r u?
zoegirl:	a smart one!

Saturday, February 5, 7:43 PM E.S.T.

zoegirl:	oh yeah, i forgot to say 1 thing.
mad maddie:	what?
zoegirl:	don't wimp out!!!

Saturday, February 5, 8:12 PM C.S.T.

SnowAngel:	zo?

Auto response from zoegirl: big things r cooking! try me later!

SnowAngel:	remember how i said i'd call again if i needed u? well, i need u.
SnowAngel:	so call me.
SnowAngel:	soon, ok?
SnowAngel:	ok. bye.

Saturday, February 5, 8:14 PM C.S.T.

SnowAngel:	maddie, thank god
mad maddie:	angela! ur a lucky girl—i just logged on for 1 sec to check msgs.
mad maddie:	zoe's been worried sick, btw. where ya been?
SnowAngel:	i ran away. i'm calling from greyhound, only i don't want anyone to hear.

Send   Cancel

mad maddie: hahaha. hence all the mystery? hence the veiled ref to bad upholstery?

mad maddie: where r u really?

SnowAngel: i really am on a greyhound. i'll be in atlanta in 12 hours.

mad maddie: a-boogie, i already told u i'm the wrong girl for yr games

mad maddie: hey, sorry for bad timing, but try me later? i luv u, can't wait to talk to u, but i'm kinda in middle of something.

SnowAngel: maddie, wait!

mad maddie: g2g. call me 2morrow!

Sunday, February 6, 10:00 AM E.S.T.

zoegirl: *shit*, maddie

mad maddie: u can say that again. 1 day—1 FREAKIN DAY—and everything comes crashing down!

zoegirl: i *knew* something was up. i just knew it! and now i feel terrible, like i should have done something to fix it all!

mad maddie: yeah, but what wld u have done? not even u cld have fixed this 1, zo.

mad maddie: wait a sec, how do u even know? oh god, the moms didn't tell your parents, did she?

zoegirl: your mom knows? how?!

mad maddie: oh let's see . . . cuz she's the 1 who had to pick me up from the police station?

zoegirl: the police station! maddie, what r u talking about?

mad maddie: what r U talking about?

zoegirl: i'm talking about *angela*! she ran away from home and she's at the bus station this very second! only i can't go pick her up cuz i'm grounded, so u have to go. and u have to go now!

mad maddie: **she's at the bus station? the ATLANTA bus station?**

mad maddie: **omg, she was telling the truth!**

zoegirl: she didn't give me the whole story cuz her battery ran out, but apparently she just couldn't take it anymore. so she hopped on a bus and traveled for 2 and a half days to get here!

mad maddie: **oh shit**

zoegirl: uh, yeah, that's what i said. and btw, why isn't *your* phone on? i've been trying to call u for the last hour!

mad maddie: **cuz as of this moment, i no longer have a phone. it's been taken away along with all my other privileges.**

mad maddie: **i got busted buying pot, zoe.**

zoegirl: oh my god

mad maddie: **um, yeah. so i'm grounded 2.**

mad maddie: **hold on—what r U grounded for?**

zoegirl: my parents came home early from the prom. they walked in on me and doug.

mad maddie: **oh no. does that mean what i think it means?**

zoegirl: it means . . . oh, man, i just can't believe this.

zoegirl: it means that altho i'm not a soiled dove, i came very close. it means that my mother saw way more of doug than she ever wanted. and it means that i'm forbidden to leave the house until i'm 43.

mad maddie: **fuck**

zoegirl: yeah

Send   Cancel

mad maddie:	**and angela's waiting at the bus station?**
zoegirl:	yeah again
zoegirl:	what r we gonna do?
mad maddie:	**well, we have no choice, do we?**
zoegirl:	but how? i seriously cannot leave the house, maddie. my mom is livid. she would physically block me from the door.
mad maddie:	**lemme think**
mad maddie:	**ok, call my land line, got it? the moms will answer, and of course she'll refuse to put me on. but that's good, cuz your job is to talk to her, not me.**
zoegirl:	talk to her about what?
mad maddie:	**about anything. use your good-girl charm and keep her chatting long enuff for me to sneak out.**
zoegirl:	how do u know she won't c u?
mad maddie:	**cuz the phone's in the kitchen and my car's parked on the street out front. if all goes well, i'll be out and back without her even knowing.**
zoegirl:	but if not, u'll be even more dead than u already r.
mad maddie:	**and so will u, cuz i guarantee my mom will call your mom.**
zoegirl:	crap
mad maddie:	**yep**
zoegirl:	well, r u ready?
mad maddie:	**zoe, i was born ready. byeas!**

Send   Cancel

207

Sunday, February 6, 11:23 AM E.S.T.

SnowAngel:	hi, zoe
zoegirl:	angela. thank god. where r u???
SnowAngel:	i had maddie drop me off at my aunt sadie's. aunt sadie is flipping out, btw. 1st she made me take a shower while she called my mom. then she made ME call my mom to reassure her that i really was alive.
zoegirl: omg.	what did your mom say? did she have any clue where u were this whole time?
SnowAngel:	of course! *huffs indignantly* what kind of daughter do u think i am?
zoegirl:	she knew u'd run off to atlanta?!
SnowAngel:	well, noooo, i didn't tell her THAT part.
SnowAngel:	thursday was the day i cut school early and bought my bus ticket, and after i did that, i called my mom and said i was spending the nite at glendy's. (as if!) i told her we had an english project to do.
zoegirl:	i *knew* u would have never gone to glendy's. that should have been my big warning sign. why didn't i listen?!
SnowAngel:	and then friday, i called and said i was gonna stay for the whole weekend since we were having such a blast.
SnowAngel:	that was a bit of irony in case u didn't notice, since it was cuz of glendy that i left in the 1st place. but i figure it's mom's own fault for believing me, cuz if she'd been paying any attention to me for the last month, she'd have known it was a big fat lie.
zoegirl:	when i talked to her, she just sounded happy that u were

Send   Cancel

off having fun. in my head i was like, "with *glendy*? i
don't think so." but i didn't say anything.

SnowAngel: i'm glad—not that it would have mattered. by that
point, there was nothing she could have done to stop
me.

zoegirl: man, angela. i can't believe u hopped on a bus and came
all the way across the country. i just can't believe it.

zoegirl: weren't u scared?

SnowAngel: i wasn't scared, exactly. it was more like everything
felt . . . unreal. like there i was, trapped in my sucky
life, and there was absolutely nothing i could do
about it, right? but then i DID do something—and it
turned out to be so much easier than i would have
thought.

zoegirl: actually, i kinda know what u mean. like after the
marshmallow incident, when i decided to just say "screw
it" to being the uptight me that i'd always been.

zoegirl: altho it is true that the uptight me would never have
been caught naked in bed with my boyfriend . . .

SnowAngel: poor zoe! i need more details on that, u know. my
phone died right when u were getting to the good
part!

zoegirl: there is no way we're gonna talk about me when u just
crossed the entire country—by yourself!—on a
greyhound. my god, angela, what was it like?

SnowAngel: like a really bad, really long field trip. mainly it was
boring, especially in states where everything looked
the same same same. instead of "wyoming," i called it
"i'm moaning." "kansas" was "can't stand us," and

Send   Cancel

	missouri was "misery." that's what i did to pass the time. i made up new names for the states i went thru. i guess it helped keep my mind off what i was doing.
zoegirl:	nobody bugged u? nobody was like, "young girl on her own—better call the cops"?
SnowAngel:	not a soul. i was still invisible, apparently.
SnowAngel:	altho there was this 1 horrible man who boarded in St. Louis. he didn't do anything gross like try to molest me, but he was big and smelly and of all the seats on the bus, he had to choose the one next to mine. his b.o. was REVOLTING, as in, i thought i was gonna barf.
zoegirl:	ick
SnowAngel:	so i got up and moved, with no excuses and no apologies. i was like, i'm not escaping the horrible glendy just to end up next to this bozo.
zoegirl:	why *did* u escape the horrible glendy? i mean, i know why in general, but what happened that day when u and i were on the phone? i heard the part where she said the 2 of u had to talk—what did she say that made u run away?
SnowAngel:	*does air-blowing-out thing so that lips make p-b-b-b-b sound*
SnowAngel:	i don't even know if i can explain. mainly it's just that i was so unhappy already, with no end in sight, and she pushed me over the edge.
zoegirl:	what did she say???
SnowAngel:	she dragged me over to a private spot on the quad, looked at me very sternly, and said, "1st of all, i'd like

Send   Cancel

	to apologize for all the things i've said to u in my head over the last few days."
zoegirl:	no!
zoegirl:	that's psycho, angela
SnowAngel:	then she said, "but i forgive u, cuz i know ur having a hard transition. your dad told my dad all about it."
zoegirl:	your dad discussed u with mr. boss?
SnowAngel:	she went on and on about how she wasn't gonna let me push her away no matter how hard i tried, cuz she knew i was just acting out of pain. and then she put her hand on my knee and leaned so close that i could smell her breath, which smelled like taco salad. she said, "i know u miss your old friends from atlanta, but they're not here. i am. and i will never leave u, i promise."
zoegirl:	ewww!
SnowAngel:	yeah
SnowAngel:	and then the reality of that hit home, how glendy was gonna be there forever and ever, and how u guys were still gonna be in atlanta. and i was like, "no. i just can't."
SnowAngel:	so . . . i left
zoegirl:	oh, angela. i don't blame u!
SnowAngel:	*puts hands on hips defiantly* and i'm glad i did, even tho i know it's gonna cause all kinds of problems. and even tho my REAL friends can't even come see me cuz ur both grounded, u idiots!
zoegirl:	shit, that's right! what in the world happened with maddie last nite? did she tell u?

SnowAngel:	yeah, and it's bad. but i'm 2 tired to explain—u'll have to IM her yourself.
zoegirl:	what? NO! tell me!
SnowAngel:	all of a sudden i can hardly keep sitting up straight. guess that's what happens after being on a bus for 3 days, huh? ttyl!

Sunday, February 6, 12:01 PM E.S.T.

zoegirl:	hey, mads. can u talk?
mad maddie:	**yeah, for a while. u rocked with the moms, dude. she has no clue i was even gone.**
zoegirl:	that's cuz i stayed on the phone with her for an entire hour!!! i was like her therapist. she was all, "i don't understand why maddie would do something like this. u would never make such bad decisions, would u, zoe?" later she asked who else of our friends "participates" in smoking marijuana, as if i was gonna give her a list.
mad maddie:	**what a freak**
zoegirl:	no, she just loves u. but the worst part was sitting there going, "uh huh, uh huh. no, i'm sure maddie doesn't have a drug problem," when i didn't even know the whole story.
zoegirl:	so while i'm very glad that u delivered angela to her aunt's, and i'm very very glad that angela herself is safe and sound, will u please tell me what happened to U last nite?
mad maddie:	**u wanna hear the story of the Big Bust? fine, but it's not pretty.**

Send   Cancel

zoegirl:	spill
mad maddie:	well, i met up with chive and whitney and brannen and meade after northside's basketball game, right? and brannen announced that he wanted some pot. so chive said, "ok, maddie and i will go buy it."
mad maddie:	now before u get all judgmental, I WASN'T PLANNING ON SMOKING ANY. but i figured it would be a good chance to get chive alone, so that we could talk.
zoegirl:	oh no. it's my fault—cuz of my dare!
mad maddie:	no, zoe, it's not your fault.
mad maddie:	actually, sure, let's make it your fault.
mad maddie:	anywayz, brannen goes, "i'll come 2," which was extremely annoying cuz i knew HE was saying it to be with ME. so then chive goes, "look, u 2 just go on. i'll stay here."
zoegirl:	aargh!
mad maddie:	yeah, but what was i supposed to say? so brannen and i took off to downtown atlanta, and at echo street i took a wrong turn, which meant that brannen ended up on the side where the sellers were, which actually turned out to be very lucky for me. so brannen bought a nickel bag, and off we drove.
zoegirl:	echo street? nickel bag? how do u know all this, maddie?
mad maddie:	do u wanna hear the story or not?
mad maddie:	5 minutes later, i looked behind me and saw a police car. i didn't think anything of it, other than to remind myself AGAIN to get my damn license.
zoegirl:	i thought u'd already gotten your new license, that day u went on your secret errand.

Send   Cancel

213

mad maddie:	nope, i blew it off cuz the line was 3 hrs long. nice move, huh?
zoegirl:	shit, maddie
mad maddie:	uh-huh, especially cuz it wasn't just a coincidence that the police were behind us. they turned on their lights and bleeped their siren, and i about crapped my pants.
zoegirl:	shit, shit, shit
mad maddie:	i pulled over, and the cops yanked me and brannen out of my car. they had us lean up against the door and they frisked us and put handcuffs on us. it was crazy. then 1 cop drove my car and the other cop drove me and brannen in the squad car, and we went to this big parking lot which was full of more cops and vans and other ppl who were obviously getting busted, just like we were.
zoegirl:	what r u saying, that it was a set-up?
mad maddie:	the guy we bought the pot from turned out to be a cop named rudolph—no lie. rudolph took our names and asked which 1 of us had bought the "oatmeal," even tho they already knew it was brannen. then the other cop asked me for my license, which of course i didn't have.
zoegirl:	poor maddie! this is terrible!
mad maddie:	they did a license check on a computer, and for some reason my license didn't come up—or maybe they just SAID it didn't. so the cop said to me, "why u lyin' to us, girl? why u lyin'?!" he was SO mean. and after a long long hassle, they said that i could go, but brannen was gonna get taken to jail. and they told me that if i was caught out on the road again, then I'D be sent to jail.

Send Cancel

zoegirl:	can they really do that? send kids to jail?
mad maddie:	**uh, guess so**
zoegirl:	but u didn't end up at jail. u ended up at the police station. i don't understand!
mad maddie:	**just chill and i'll explain. SO . . . i drove back to chive's and told everyone the story, and then chive and i took off to get brannen out of jail.**
zoegirl:	maddie, no!!!
mad maddie:	**but we had an unbelievably hard time trying to figure out where brannen was, and we drove around downtown atlanta for like 2 hours before finding the holding cell. turns out brannen's bail was $1,500.00, which meant that the bond would be $150.00. but we only had $98.00, cuz that's all we'd collected back at chive's. the bondsman we talked to told us that we needed to get the rest of the money and then come back with someone over 24 who had a responsible job. THEN he'd give us the bond.**
zoegirl:	good god, maddie. u know all this weird stuff that i would never in a million years dream of knowing.
mad maddie:	**well believe me, i'd rather not. so we decided to drive to dunwoody and get my cousin donovan, only as we were walking back to my car we heard a man yell, "hey! you two! get over here!"**
zoegirl:	oh no. what now?
mad maddie:	**it was the exact same cops who had busted me and brannen after we bought the oatmeal from rudolph. i couldn't fucking believe it. they took us to the station and made us call our parents—and THAT'S why i'm grounded.**

Send Cancel

zoegirl:	ugh, what a mess. what an awful, awful mess.
mad maddie:	**except there is one last thing. i did finish the dare.**
zoegirl:	hold on. somehow in the middle of this, u found time to have your heart-to-heart with chive?
mad maddie:	**we were sitting on this hard metal bench outside the police station, and i thought, "well, things sure as hell can't get any worse."**
mad maddie:	**actually, what i REALLY thought, cuz i'm an idiot, is that we were having, like, this big moment. we were going thru this really shitty thing, but at least we were going thru it together.**
zoegirl:	so . . . what did u say?
mad maddie:	**i told him that i liked him—more than just as a friend.**
zoegirl:	and?
mad maddie:	**well, it's not good.**
mad maddie:	**he put his head in his hands and said, "ahh, maddie." like he was in pain.**
zoegirl:	uh oh
mad maddie:	**he goes, "maddie . . . i'm with whitney." my heart was pounding really hard, but i made myself say, "why?" meaning, she doesn't get u. she can't keep up with u, she doesn't even get your jokes.**
zoegir1l:	but *u* do
mad maddie:	**yeah, i do, and he KNOWS that, zoe. i could c it in his eyes. but he just shook his head really mournfully. he said, "i'm probably making a big mistake, huh?"**
zoegirl:	like that's supposed to make it better? don't be man enuff to actually *act* on it, just toss it out there like a consolation prize?

Send   Cancel

zoegirl:	he doesn't deserve u, maddie.
mad maddie:	**then he took my hand and gave me one of his soul-piercing looks and said, "we can still spend time together, tho. nothing has to change."**
zoegirl:	does "spending time together" mean "fooling around"?
zoegirl:	i hope u told him where to shove it.
mad maddie:	**then my parents drove up, and that was that.**
mad maddie:	**the moms is so bent, btw. in fact i have to go, cuz she just knocked on my door and said in this pinched voice that she wants to talk to me. guess it's time for lecture #3 on The Evil of Drugs.**
zoegirl:	maddie, i am so so so so sorry
mad maddie:	**just another sucky day in suck land.**
mad maddie:	**u know what, tho?**
zoegirl:	what?
mad maddie:	**i am glad i told him, cuz now i know.**

Sunday, February 6, 7:33 PM E.S.T.

zoegirl:	hey there, sleepyhead
SnowAngel:	hey, zo. my aunt told me u called a couple of times, but she didn't wanna wake me. sorry.
zoegirl:	that's ok, i just wanted to check in and c how u were doing.
SnowAngel:	about like this, i'd say.
zoegirl:	what's that, u with tire tracks across your face?
SnowAngel:	i just got off the phone with my mom. she said she's really upset with me for running away, but that she's

Send   Cancel

	also really upset that she didn't know how unhappy i was living in el cerrito. i was like, "mom, u didn't know cuz u didn't WANT to know."
zoegirl:	is she gonna make u go back?
SnowAngel:	NO, cuz i refuse to. i told her that flat out, and she said, "angela, ur our daughter. u'll do what we say." *rolls eyes*
zoegirl:	so what does that mean?
SnowAngel:	we're in negotiation. let's put it that way.
zoegirl:	what about school?
SnowAngel:	well, if i stay here with aunt sadie, i'll go back to school with u guys. but not tomorrow. not till everything gets settled 1 way or another.
zoegirl:	wow. i am so impressed with u, angela. i really am.
SnowAngel:	what about u—how's life on the home front?
zoegirl:	ehh . . .
zoegirl:	on the bright side, i didn't run away, and i didn't get busted buying pot. on the un-bright side, my mother saw my boyfriend's naked butt.
SnowAngel:	the dark side of the moon, like that pink floyd song. hee hee.
zoegirl:	i'm glad u can laff about it
zoegirl:	it's just so ridiculous, my mom coming home from the prom and catching me and doug going at it. and poor doug! he sent me an email saying he's never stepping foot in my house again.
SnowAngel:	and ur never stepping foot out of your house again, if your mom has anything to say about it. which will make things tricky, huh?

Send   Cancel

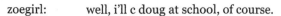

zoegirl:	well, i'll c doug at school, of course.
zoegirl:	u know what's weird? i'm not glad that mom walked in on us, obviously, but at the same time . . .
SnowAngel:	at the same time what?
zoegirl:	here's the thing. we stopped cuz my mom barged in on us. and if she hadn't . . . i don't know what would have happened. and that kinda scares me, cuz as u know, i wasn't planning on that.
SnowAngel:	whoa
zoegirl:	and who knows, maybe it wouldn't have happened anyway. it probably wouldn't have.
SnowAngel:	this time u really r talking about sex, right? about u and doug going all the way?
zoegirl:	we didn't even have condoms, angela. it would have been bad.
SnowAngel:	r u gonna buy some for next time?
zoegirl:	there's not gonna *be* a next time for a very long time. i'm sure my mom's gonna make it hard for me and doug to be alone together, even when i'm not grounded anymore. *if* i'm ever not grounded anymore.
SnowAngel:	and how do u feel about this? *raises eyebrows inquiringly*
zoegirl:	frustrated? relieved?
zoegirl:	i dunno
zoegirl:	the whole nite—until mom busted in—was amazing. and my body wanted more and more and more. but deep down i'm just not ready.
SnowAngel:	how does doug feel about it?

Send   Cancel

zoegirl:	he's like me—at least he says he is. altho part of me thinks that if i said, "yes, let's go for it," he'd agree right away.
SnowAngel:	nooooo, really?
zoegirl:	i do love him, angela. it's just all so confusing.
SnowAngel:	don't i know it—not just boys, but EVERYTHING!

Sunday, February 6, 10:01 PM E.S.T.

mad maddie:	**hey, u. i thought u'd be conked by now.**
SnowAngel:	i took a long nap. plus, my body's still on california time. it's only 7 in el cerrito. isn't that weird?
mad maddie:	**do u wish u were back there?**
SnowAngel:	r u kidding??? not in the slightest.
SnowAngel:	i'm sure i'll miss my mom and dad and chrissy eventually, but no, i don't wish i was there.
mad maddie:	**well, maybe i should take your place. think your parents would notice?**
SnowAngel:	madigan kinnick! *puts hands on hips* i came all this way to be with U. don't even tease me like that.
mad maddie:	**i just need a break from the moms, that's all. she can't get it into her head that my pot smoking days r over, that they were over even before the Big Bust.**
mad maddie:	**the theme of tonite's lecture was that she thinks i have a "naive" philosophy toward life, which is that i have to try something out before i can make a decision about it. so she goes, "but u don't need to rob a bank to know that's bad, now do u? poison little children? put glass in halloween candy?"**

SnowAngel:	good grief
mad maddie:	**she also thinks that i was pressured into smoking, that chive made me do it. i told her, "why do u insist on believing that i can't possibly make a decision on my own? no one 'persuaded' me to do anything. it was not peer pressure!"**
SnowAngel:	huh. i'm not sure that's the angle i would have taken . . .
mad maddie:	**the moms just shook her head and said, "i don't believe that, maddie. i simply don't believe that."**
mad maddie:	**aaargh**
SnowAngel:	what about chive and brannen? have u heard from them?
mad maddie:	**brannen's mom went down to the jail and got him. he's grounded, just like me, plus he has to do 40 hours of community service. chive got off scott free except for being yelled at by his mom. but i didn't talk to him for long, cuz it made me feel 2 weird.**
mad maddie:	**i'm glad they go to n'side so i don't have to c either of them at school tomorrow.**
SnowAngel:	as for me, i don't have to go to school at all. vacation day! vacation day!
mad maddie:	**lucky dog**
mad maddie:	**will u do me a favor, then? i'd do it myself, but i can't, obviously.**
SnowAngel:	what is it?
mad maddie:	**i need u to go to 2620 moreland avenue. ask for a guy named willy.**
SnowAngel:	excuse me? who's willy?
mad maddie:	**tell him ur picking up the package for madigan kinnick.**

Send   Cancel   221

	it's already paid for, so u don't have to worry.
SnowAngel:	maddie . . . what kind of errand r u sending me on? i thought u were done with your life of crime!
mad maddie:	**oh please. yeah, willy sells pot from behind the cash register, and i'm sending u to get it.**
mad maddie:	**give me a little credit, will ya?**
SnowAngel:	what is it, then?
mad maddie:	**don't open it until i tell u to. there's 1 for u, 1 for zoe, and 1 for me.**
SnowAngel:	a surprise? 😁 i love surprises!
mad maddie:	**so u'll do it?**
SnowAngel:	of course. i have to go out anyway, cuz i need to buy a new charger for my cell phone. my aunt's gonna let me use her mini cooper.
mad maddie:	**a mini cooper, nice.**
SnowAngel:	i know. it's even cuter than a VW bug. *big thumbs up*
mad maddie:	**IM me tomorrow after school. c yas!**

Monday, February 7, 4:05 PM E.S.T.

SnowAngel:	IMPORTANT MESSAGE TO U FROM ME
mad maddie:	**yes?**
SnowAngel:	i have picked up the "surprises" per your instructions. i have delivered 1 to zoe and 1 to u, which your mom should have given to u now that ur home from school. did she?
mad maddie:	**i've got the box right here. u haven't opened yours yet, have u?**

Send   Cancel

SnowAngel: no, but i am extremely tempted!

SnowAngel: neither zoe nor i can hold on much longer, so i'm
             setting up our chatroom so that we can open them
             together. okey-dokey?

mad maddie: bring it on!

You have just entered the room "Angela's Boudoir."
mad maddie has entered the room.
zoegirl has entered the room.

SnowAngel: hola, girls!

zoegirl: hi, angela. maddie, u there?

mad maddie: howdy, friends

mad maddie: does everyone have her box?

zoegirl: what is it? tell us!

mad maddie: 1, 2, 3, open!

SnowAngel: omg!!! *squeals and jumps up and down in a frenzy!*

zoegirl: maddie, it's beautiful!

mad maddie: yeah, yeah, yeah. i know.

SnowAngel: oh, mads, it's just like the one i lost!!!

SnowAngel: do both of yours say "believe," 2?

zoegirl: mine does

**mad maddie: mine 2. aren't i corny, getting us matching bracelets? i am
             so corny i can hardly believe it.**

SnowAngel: i love it sooo much!

zoegirl: me 2, me 2!

SnowAngel: but i'm confused. my original bracelet didn't come

	from that store on moreland ave. it came from curiosities. and zoe, didn't u go back to curiosities after i moved? and they didn't have any more!
zoegirl:	that's true, they were all sold out.
mad maddie:	**listen, girl. when u want something bad enuff, u MAKE it happen.**
SnowAngel:	but how???
mad maddie:	**dude, i went to every single store in little five points, and NOBODY had any "believe" bracelets. finally this lady told me to talk to willy at a store called moon daughter, cuz he's a silversmith and he makes stuff like that. so i told willy what i wanted, i even drew him a little picture, and he said, "sure, i can do that."**
SnowAngel:	aw, maddie, ur the best friend ever!
mad maddie:	**no, u r!**
SnowAngel:	no, U r!
zoegirl:	hey—what about ME?
SnowAngel:	*gives zoe a noogie* and u r 2, of course
SnowAngel:	we're ALL the best friends ever! *melts into a mush pile of affection*
mad maddie:	**i put the order in for the bracelets a long time ago—back when u were still in california, angela. i wanted to cheer u up, u know? i hated that i couldn't do anything to make things better for u.**
mad maddie:	**but then u made things better for yourself. ur a stud, girl.**
SnowAngel:	u know why, tho, right? cuz of u and zoe. if u guys were willing to take control of your lives, then i should be, 2.
mad maddie:	**fat lot of good it did us. we're both grounded!**

Send   Cancel

SnowAngel:	well, guess what? *giggles behind hand* i am 2!
mad maddie:	**wtf?**
SnowAngel:	i told zoe already, when i dropped off her bracelet. zoe, tell maddie.
zoegirl:	she's grounded at her aunt's house, supposedly until the end of time. but we think her sentence will eventually be lifted. it's mainly just angela's parents' way of proving they can be long-distance parents.
mad maddie:	**long-distance parents?**
mad maddie:	**what r u saying?**
zoegirl:	she can stay!!!
SnowAngel:	i can stay!!! 😁😁😁
mad maddie:	**r u serious?**
SnowAngel:	i am the epitome of all seriousness. i have grown a beard, that's how serious i am. i will only wear tweed, with leather elbow-patches.
mad maddie:	**u r punch drunk**
SnowAngel:	*twirls about giddily* it's true, i am. i'm drunk on magnolia trees and my aunt sadie's mini cooper and true blue friends forever and ever. ☺
mad maddie:	**ok, i'm still trying to soak this in. your parents said, "sure, u can live in atlanta"? just like that?**
zoegirl:	just for spring semester, and then they'll re-evaluate. if things don't work out, or if angela's aunt says there's a problem, then angela gets shipped back pronto. but that's not gonna happen.
SnowAngel:	especially since i'll have u 2 to keep me straight. after all, ur SUCH good influences.
zoegirl:	haha

Send   Cancel

225

mad maddie:	**maybe it's good that we're all locked in our respective houses, huh? at least it'll keep us out of trouble.**
mad maddie:	**in fact, i dare say . . . yes, yes . . . this calls for a googlewhack!**
SnowAngel:	what r u gonna try? "grounded girlies"?
zoegirl:	"punished pals"?
SnowAngel:	"caged cuties"?
mad maddie:	**ok, stop. ur starting to sound pornographic.**
mad maddie:	**i've got it, "virtuous rebels." cuz that's really what we r, right?**
SnowAngel:	and what's the verdict?
mad maddie:	**damn! 37,100 hits!**
mad maddie:	**will i ever find the one???**
zoegirl:	i found the one, and it's doug.
mad maddie:	**i meant "the one" googlewhack, idiot. as in, the googlewhack that results in just 1 hit. must it all be about doug?**
zoegirl:	i'm sorry, i'm sorry. it's just that it's only been 2 days of being grounded, and already i miss him so much!
SnowAngel:	oh, poo. stop being so dramatic.
zoegirl:	me, dramatic? ur calling *me* dramatic?
mad maddie:	**quit yer whining. u'll c him saturday nite at kidding around, won't u?**
zoegirl:	yes, only my mom has informed me that she'll be dropping me off and picking me up so that there's no "unsupervised contact." it's a nightmare.
mad maddie:	**u want a nightmare, try living at my house. the moms honestly and truly held up an egg this morning and said,**

Send   Cancel

	"this is your brain." then she cracked it into the skillet. "this is your brain on drugs."
SnowAngel:	mmm, scrambled eggs ¦☺¦
SnowAngel:	now that the weight of the world is off my shoulders, i'm starting to get my appetite back.
zoegirl:	doug did something cute at school, tho. he gave me a hug, and without telling me, he slipped a bendy heart into my jacket pocket. it has little rubber arms and little rubber legs and a glued-on picture of his face where the head would be.
SnowAngel:	awwww!
mad maddie:	**retch, retch**
zoegirl:	he wrote me another poem, 2. it's about how he values our friendship just as much, if not more, than all this other stuff. it ends like this:

> But for now just let me hold you close
> As I hear your breath and feel your sighs,
> And let me take a healthy dose
> Of your essence, smile, soul, and eyes.

SnowAngel:	that's so sweet!
zoegirl:	isn't it?
SnowAngel:	*jabs maddie in shoulder* don't u have anything to add, mads?
mad maddie:	**er . . . what angela said**
zoegirl:	maddie! i *know* ur rolling your eyes, so u can just stop.
zoegirl:	but i don't even care, cuz i know there's something b/w us. he really is the one.

Send   Cancel

227

SnowAngel:	i think that's great, zoe
mad maddie:	**it IS great. i thought i had that with chive, but obviously i don't.**
SnowAngel:	*puts arm around maddie sympathetically*
zoegirl:	anyway, i've just been thinking a lot about it . . . and my honest prediction is that we will, u know, make love.
SnowAngel:	*lets out low whistle*
zoegirl:	just not anytime soon, obviously
mad maddie:	**unless u do it in the supply closet at Kidding Around . . .**
zoegirl:	maddie!
mad maddie:	**jk**
mad maddie:	**i, on the other hand, will NOT be getting any action in the near future, cuz i called chive from the school's pay phone and told him that we're done fooling around. now there's a twist, huh?**
SnowAngel:	maddie, omg! i am SO proud of u!
mad maddie:	**well, it's like my dad says. why buy the cow if u can have the milk for free?**
zoegirl:	yes, absolutely. and u'll *know* when it's real, mads, u really will. just like i do with doug.
mad maddie:	**yeah, shut up. that sounds a little 2 much like rubbing it in.**
zoegirl:	maddie, no! i'm not trying to rub it in at all!
mad maddie:	**whatevs**
mad maddie:	**but we've discussed it enuff, ok? it's not easy, even tho i know it's the right thing to do.**
mad maddie:	**i always learn my fucking life lessons the hard way.**
SnowAngel:	ah, mads. but at least u've got us.

Send   Cancel

mad maddie: **so . . . u guys really like your bracelets? really and truly?**

SnowAngel: i love mine. i completely and fully love it.

zoegirl: me 2. i can't wait to c what it looks like on.

mad maddie: **OH! that reminds me. the rule is that we have to put them on for each other. none of this "bracelet breakthrough, i-don't-need-anyone-but-myself" business, got it?**

zoegirl: huh?

SnowAngel: she's talking about this great method i invented of putting bracelets on.

SnowAngel: but she's right. her way is better.

zoegirl: that means we can't wear them until we're all together, tho.

mad maddie: **true**

mad maddie: **but no worries, we'll find a way around this foolish grounding business.**

SnowAngel: surely your parents will let u come c ME, won't they? dear pitiful me who's been gone for so long?

SnowAngel: my aunt sadie could be our chaperone and make sure that no one smokes pot or does the nasty. ☺

zoegirl: haha, very funny

SnowAngel: ahhh, my friends. i think things r looking up.

mad maddie: **yeah, life is good, even when it sucks.**

zoegirl: we'll c each other soon, then?

SnowAngel: very soon. so altho i'm signing off—*draws hand to heart emotionally*—it is with the comfort of knowing that it is the most temporary of farewells.

zoegirl: u make me laff, angela. but yeah, i should go 2.

mad maddie:	**laters, dudes**
SnowAngel:	and btw, i DO believe! i do, i do!
mad maddie:	**u sound like tinkerbell, u nut**
SnowAngel:	*wiggles cute little bottom suggestively*
SnowAngel:	ttfn!!!

Send   Cancel

About the Author

Of writing *ttfn*, Lauren says, "The coolest things was getting to incorporate the crazy stories and funky vocab that my readers passed on when they emailed me. Like 'diesel,' as in, 'That's so diesel!' And 'crudballs.' What's not to love about 'crudballs'? I had so much fun writing this novel. Here's hoping it's equally fun to read!"

Lauren is also the author of *ttyl*; *l8r, g8r*; and *Rhymes with Witches*. She holds an MFA in Writing for Children and Young Adults from Vermont College and lives with her family in Colorado. You can catch up with her—in fact she really hopes you will!—at www.laurenmyracle.com.

The text in this book is set in 10-point Georgia, TheSans 9-Black, and ComicSans. The cell phone icons and many of the smiley faces were created by Celina Carvalho.

Enjoy this sneak peek at
Lauren Myracle's sequel to *ttyl* and *ttfn*:

l8r, g8r

Tuesday, February 7, 5:17 PM

SnowAngel:	mads, thank goodness i caught u
SnowAngel:	i'm not going to the airport after all, k?
mad maddie:	**angela! i was JUST about to log off and come get u, and now i'm staring at u dumbfounded.**
mad maddie:	**of course ur coming. zoe's expecting u!**
SnowAngel:	but c, doug's HER boyfriend, right? why does she need us to go with her to the airport?
mad maddie:	**uh, cuz she's zoe?**
mad maddie:	**and cuz she hasn't seen the guy for a whole semester. more, if u add the time we spent in california over summer break. we got back, and she saw him for . . . what? a grand total of 1 week before he took off in his sailor suit to "Sea the World"?**
SnowAngel:	r we doing that again? making fun of the name?
mad maddie:	**yes, cuz it demands to be made fun of!**
mad maddie:	**seriously, who goes to "Sea the World" during the 1st semester of their senior yr? senior yr is a time for madcap partying, not for sailing about the globe and stuffing yourself with culture.**

Send   Cancel

SnowAngel:	+coughs+ on a party boat under jet blue skies, surrounded by girls in bikinis. . .
mad maddie:	**like i said. what was he thinking?**
SnowAngel:	i saw a "sex and the city" rerun last nite where carrie meets these guys in the navy, and they were hot in their sailor suits. u wouldn't think it, but they were.
mad maddie:	**i don't think doug would be hot in a sailor suit.**
SnowAngel:	well . . . no
SnowAngel:	but hot or not, i'm not going to be there to c him. it's not that i don't WANT to, it's just that
mad maddie:	**yesssssssss?**
SnowAngel:	i have a flesh-eating virus.
SnowAngel:	i DO!
mad maddie:	**excusez-moi?**
SnowAngel:	i have a flesh-eating virus and it is attacking my nose and i am DISFIGURED.
SnowAngel:	don't u dare laff!
mad maddie:	**angela, i saw u at school and u were fine**
SnowAngel:	but it was beginning. i could feel it.
mad maddie:	**uh huh. and where did u get this flesh-eating virus?**
mad maddie:	**does it by any chance have to do with the fact that we're talking about doug?**
SnowAngel:	what? NO!
mad maddie:	**r u sure? cuz i know u, angela. don't think i've forgotten your whole "doug will be my starter husband" spiel.**
SnowAngel:	maddie, that was LAST YEAR, way before doug and zoe even started dating.

Send   Cancel   237

SnowAngel:	anyway, did u happen to forget the 1 small fact that i'm going out with logan now???
mad maddie:	**ohhhh, right. logan.**
SnowAngel:	+puts hands on hips+ why do u say it that way?
mad maddie:	**what way?**
SnowAngel:	u know what way
mad maddie:	**and U know why. so drop it.**
mad maddie:	**i think it's interesting that u develop a flesh-eating virus on the very day ur supposed to c doug, that's all.**
SnowAngel:	u think i'm making it up? i'm not making it up, maddie. if u insist on being technical, it's a staph infection. it's all nasty under my nose—and even up INSIDE my nose so that it looks very booger-ish and vile—and i'm not going out in public looking like this!
mad maddie:	**wait a sec—a memory is intruding**
mad maddie:	**didn't this same staph infection thing happen last yr?**
SnowAngel:	yes +sniff, sniff+
SnowAngel:	it happens every year when i get a bad cold, and now i'll have to go on antibiotics and it'll take a week to clear up and until then everyone will think i've got a huge booger oozing out of my right nostril. they'll call me booger girl! that's what it'll say in the senior section of the yearbook. angela silver: booger girl!
mad maddie:	**god, ur vain**
SnowAngel:	ur calling me VAIN?!! +pops a blood vessel in outrage+
SnowAngel:	of COURSE i'm vain. i've been vain my entire life!
mad maddie:	**so then suck it up and come with us to the airport!**

Send   Cancel

SnowAngel:	let me describe exactly what i'm talking about so u get the full picture. it's an OPEN SORE under my nostril. it's red and bubbly and slimy with neosporin, and it's growing even as we speak.
SnowAngel:	it PULSES, maddie
mad maddie:	**what is it with u and things that pulse?**
SnowAngel:	???
mad maddie:	**oh, angela, don't even! 1) your staph infection pulses. 2) u can't bear to touch your wrist cuz the vein there pulses. and 3), dear god, we certainly can't forget your neck.**
mad maddie:	**"woe is me, i can feel my blood pulsing thru my pillow! it jams up wrong against my carotid artery!"**
SnowAngel:	WELL IT DOES
mad maddie:	**then get a new one. (pillow, not neck, heh heh heh.) u've been complaining about it for frickin ever!**
SnowAngel:	+adopts a wounded expression+ i have had a series of unfortunate pillows, thank u very much. aunt sadie is a sweetie, but her pillows r crap. that's the only bad thing about living with her.
mad maddie:	**that and the fact that she burns every single thing she tries to cook.**
SnowAngel:	well, true
mad maddie:	**and she's a shopaholic.**
SnowAngel:	TINY shopaholic. small insignificant problem.
mad maddie:	**ur parents have no idea what they've gotten u into, do they?**
SnowAngel:	my parents think that aunt sadie is taking very good care of me, which she is!

Send   Cancel

SnowAngel:	anyway, don't u have somewhere to go? shouldn't u be leaving now?
mad maddie:	**yeah, guess i better. u really don't wanna come?**
SnowAngel:	it's not that i don't—it's that i can't. now scat, cat!
mad maddie:	**all right. but remind me to tell u about the latest jana drama, which zoe was unfortunate enuff to witness.**
SnowAngel:	call me after u drop off zoe and doug
mad maddie:	**u got it. bye, booger girl!**

Send   Cancel

Keep reading! If you liked this book, check out these other titles.

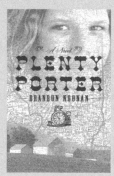